THE 2024 OFF BROAD STREET SHORT PLAY FESTIVAL

THE 2024 OFF BROAD STREET SHORT PLAY FESTIVAL

© 2024. All rights reserved.

Cover & Book Design: Jonathan Cook
First Edition: March 2024
ISBN: 978-1-7375216-7-9

The 2024 Off Broad Street Short Play Festival took place in April 2024 at Le Chat Noir Theatre in Augusta, GA.

From a total of 767 submissions, the 9 plays within this anthology were the top plays selected to be produced in the festival.

Table of Contents

A GOOD FIT

by Jaclyn Stiller

Two women visit a coffee shop. One is there for a job interview. The other for a blind date. Unfortunately, they accidentally sit at the wrong tables. (Comedy, 2M, 2W)

CHARACTERS

JOHN
Male, 20-30's; whose life is as interesting as his quarterly finance report.

TESSA
Female, 20s-30s; sarcastic and smart, trying to be more open minded.

JON
Male, 20s-30s; finally ready to start dating again.

SHANNON
Female, 20s-30s; Type A, determined to make a good first impression.

SETTING

Your everyday coffee shop. At least two tables, each with two chairs.

<u>Suggested blocking:</u>
Table 1: John & Tessa
Table 2: Shannon & Jon
Tessa and Shannon have their backs to each other.

NOTES

--- indicates a shift in focus from one table to the other

A GOOD FIT by Jaclyn Stiller

***

At rise, John sits at a table alone with his laptop open, coffee in hand, and on the phone.

JOHN. The quarterly numbers should be in your inbox. *(Pause.)* It was an attachment. *(Pause.)* There it is. Hey, any news on when they'll be done fumigating the office? *(Long pause.)* No, yeah, it's fine, I'm just working from a coffee shop. *(Pause.)* Yes, I've scheduled interviews to find the new admin assistant. I got the first one in a few minutes. Okay, we can circle back end-of-day. *(He hangs up. Tessa enters, glances around briefly, then gets a phone call.)*

TESSA. Hey. No, I haven't seen him yet. His profile just had a bunch of pictures of him in a hat. *(Pause.)* No that doesn't mean he's bald! He could just really like hats. Plus it's perfectly fine to be bald. Listen, if this date goes south, I'm going to need you to fake an emergency. Here goes nothing. *(She hangs up; sees JOHN and walks over to him.)* Hi, are you Jon?

JOHN. Hi, yes! Please take a seat.

TESSA. Not bald, thank God.

JOHN. Sorry?

TESSA. Nothing. You look nice.

JOHN. Oh, um, thank you. Give me one second to pull up my questions.

TESSA. You brought questions?

JOHN. Of course. *(Fiddles with laptop.)* First question, tell me a little bit about yourself.

TESSA. Sure. Well, I'm originally from New Jersey, but I moved here for school and I've been here ever since. I have a cat named Meatball. I'm the youngest of four siblings. I love photography, true crime, concerts, painting … hmm, anything critical that I'm forgetting … oh! And I'm a Gemini.

JOHN. *(Pause.)* Okay. Nice to see a wide range of interests. And tell me about your education experience.

TESSA. Right, that! I majored in Psychology with an English minor. What about you?

JOHN. Me? I hold a business degree, and I'm currently pursuing my MBA. *(Jon enters carrying two full coffee cups and sits at another table.)* So, psychology degree. What makes you think you would be a good fit?

TESSA. Excuse me?

JOHN. What makes you think you would be well suited? I'm looking for someone who is highly flexible and willing to try new things.

TESSA. Oh, that's very … forward of you. Don't you think it's a little early to be discussing those things?

JOHN. I suppose so. *(Shannon enters in a rush, hurries over to Jon.)*

SHANNON. Hi, are you John? So sorry I'm late, I had to cut across town.

JON. Hi! Yeah, no worries. *(Stands, goes for a hug; Shannon goes for a handshake. They settle on a handshake.)*

SHANNON. I've been really looking forward to meeting with you.

JON. Really? Gosh, that's nice. I've been looking forward to this too. I got to say, you look a little different than I was expecting.

SHANNON. Oh? Well, you can't judge a book by its LinkedIn photo.

JON. Totally … *(They sit down. Awkward silence.)*

SHANNON. So, did you have any questions for me?

JON. Oh! Right, sorry it's been a while since I've done one of these. Um, tell me about you.

SHANNON. I'd love to. I'm a graduate of the U, where I studied Communications and Business Management. I exhibited leadership and public speaking skills as a campus tour guide, and I gained additional corporate experience as an intern at the City Hall office. I also spent a semester studying abroad in Ireland to enrich my international perspectives. And my skills include organization, time management, and Microsoft Excel.

JON. Wow. Well … those are quite the accomplishments.

SHANNON. Thank you. I find that I thrive in environments that challenge me to think on my feet and collaborate with others.

JON. So like, pickleball?

JOHN. Next question. What is your biggest weakness?

TESSA. Oof, my therapist would probably say it's my avoidant attachment style, but I'd argue it's more just a classic fear of commitment. *(John makes no response but types on his laptop.)* Are you actually writing that down?

JOHN. And where do you see yourself in five years?

TESSA. Oh God, this question.

JOHN. You don't like it?

TESSA. I just think it's a silly question. It assumes that I know where I should be going and how to get there. Five years ago, I was studying to be a chemical engineer, until I realized I hated chemistry. I was just doing it for my parents. I don't know, dreams change. I mean, c'mon. Childhood-you must have had some other dream job before you decided to be an MBA.

JOHN. Nope, I always dreamed of being a Senior Corporate Strategic Analyst-comma-North America Region.

TESSA. Makes sense, it seems like such noble work. If you don't analyze those spreadsheets, who will?

JOHN. You're right. No one would ever know how we did on our key performance indicators!

TESSA. It would be a tragedy! *(They share a smile.)*

JON. Okay, here's a fun question. If your friends had to pick one word that reminds them of you, what would it be?

SHANNON. Hmm. Anal. *(Jon chokes on coffee.)* But don't worry! I can be very flexible, and I come with a lot of experience.

JON. That's … wow. That's great. Not that I need you to have a lot of experience! I just, good for you.

SHANNON. Aren't you going to ask me about them?

JON. About what?

SHANNON. My past experiences.

JON. Oh! I don't know if we need to get into all that. Unless there's something you really want to tell me. But I feel like we should get to know each other a little better before we start talking about our exes.

SHANNON. I'm sorry, I'm confused.

JOHN. I should really mention, the last person left because of challenges with punctuality. To put it frankly, she always struggled to come on time. Will that be an issue for you?

TESSA. Will coming on time be an issue for me??

JON. I'm sorry. I promised myself I wouldn't bring up Hannah. It's just that she and I had a really good thing going until she left … but I promise you I'm over her completely!

SHANNON. And Hannah was the previous admin assistant?

TESSA. Why would you ask me something like that?

JON. No, we were dating. But I was told never to mention exes on a first date.

JOHN. That's a very normal question for a job interview!

TESSA. *(Together.)* This is a job interview??

SHANNON. *(Together.)* This is a date?? (Tessa and Shannon gasp and turn to look at each other, realizing what the other person just said.)*

TESSA. I think I have the wrong Jon.

SHANNON. I think I have your Jon. *(Tessa and Shannon ad lib over each other as they gather their things and switch places. "I'm so sorry"/"This is awkward"/"His profile was really vague!"/"Why is every guy named John?")*

SHANNON. I am so sorry, I think I'm meant to be interviewing with you today. My name is Shannon Hofland.

TESSA. Hi, you're Jon from Bumble right? I'm Tessa.

JOHN. Um, yes I'm not sure what just happened. Give me one second, I need to straighten out my notes.

JON. Oh, you're Tessa! That makes so much more sense.

TESSA. Yeah, sorry for the confusion!

JON. I was beginning to feel very underqualified.

JOHN. Okay Shannon, why don't we start with you telling me about yourself.

SHANNON. Well, I'm a graduate of the U, where I studied Communications and Business Management. I exhibited leadership and public speaking skills when I was a campus tour guide, and I gained additional corporate experience ... *(Continues speaking silently, meanwhile John's eyes drift back to Tessa.)*

JON. That's a good question. My desert island movie would have to be ... *The Dark Knight*, for sure.

TESSA. I've never seen it.

JON. What? Oh my gosh, you have to watch it. Christopher Nolan is such a genius. He like, completely redefined the superhero genre. He made it so much more dark and gritty. And Heath Ledger is the perfect Joker! *(Continues rambling silently.)*

JOHN. And why do you believe you would be a good fit as an admin assistant?

SHANNON. Like I said earlier, I thrive in fast-paced environments that challenge me to adapt. Or, maybe I said that to the other guy ... nevertheless, I believe my strong organizational skills and attention to detail perfectly align with the demands of this role.

JOHN. Great.

JON. See, the coolest thing about Christopher Nolan is that he doesn't use CGI. It's all practical effects. And then you pair that with all the mind-bending narratives and the theoretical physics – did you know he didn't even study physics?

TESSA. No, I didn't.

JON. He's such a genius. His movies are just ... masterpieces. We should watch one sometime.

TESSA. *(Looking at her phone in her lap.)* For sure. Wait, what did you say?

SHANNON. My biggest weakness is probably that I'm too much of a perfectionist. My friends have even called me anal – oh, I heard it. *(Beat.)* Anyway, I just can't stand it when things aren't absolutely perfect.

JOHN. Yeah, I'm sure that must be a challenge for you. So, where do you see yourself in five – *(Hesitates, then closes the laptop.)*. Tell me something about you that isn't on your resume.

SHANNON. Like what?

JOHN. Anything. What's something about you that's not on your resume, but is a part of who you are?

SHANNON. *(Beat.)* I tap dance.

JOHN. Tap dance?

SHANNON. I did it competitively in college, now just for fun. I like that it's structured. Every movement has a distinct purpose. And when you put it all together and look at it, you realize you're actually a percussionist as well as a dancer. You're a part of the song. But I don't know what that has to do with being an admin assistant.

JOHN. I don't either. But that's really neat.

TESSA. *(Getting up to leave.)* I'm so sorry, that was my roommate on the phone. Apparently, my cat is having an asthma attack. She has feline bronchitis. *(Forgets her purse on the chair.)*

JON. Oh, I hope everything's alright. Should I call you?

TESSA. *(Edging away.)* Um, don't worry about it. I'll be in touch. *(She exits.)*

JON. It was really nice meeting you! *(To himself.)* I think that went well. *(He exits.)*

JOHN. Those are all the questions I have for you. It was a pleasure meeting you today, Shannon, despite our little mix up earlier.

SHANNON. Yes, I feel bad for the girl who didn't realize she was in a job interview.

JOHN. She actually did alright. She was funny. *(Beat.)* Well, you'll be hearing from us in a week or two. Thank you again for coming in.

SHANNON. Thank you, have a nice day. *(She exits. John starts packing up his laptop. Tessa enters and walks back to the chair she was last in. John sees her and waves.)*

TESSA. Forgot my purse. How was your interview?

JOHN. Good, I think she'll be a good fit. How was your date?

TESSA. We've decided to go in a different direction.

JOHN. Sorry to hear that.

TESSA. *(Beat.)* Well, bye.

JOHN. Actually – if you're still accepting other candidates, would you possibly consider …? *(Gestures vaguely at himself.)*

TESSA. Yeah, okay. *(They sit down together. Tessa extends a handshake.)* Nice to meet you, John.

JOHN. Nice to meet you too…um?

TESSA. Tessa.

JOHN. Tessa.

TESSA. So, tell me about yourself.

END OF PLAY

BABBLE

by Zachary Pareizs

An intergalactic reconnaissance team are exploring what they thought was an uninhabited planet. When one of them is attacked by a creature on the surface, they find that the infection that follows disrupts their human communication. (Sci-fi, Horror, 1M, 3W)

CHARACTERS

NORA
Female; Mechanic, poet, runs the ship.

ESTHER
Female; Bright ecological scientist. Married to Noah.

STEPHEN
Male; Slightly dopey but earnest geologist. Self-identifies as a wife guy.

MARY
*Female AI operating system that flies and operates the ship. Possibly sentient. *Only her voice is heard in the play.*

SETTING

The control room of a reconnaissance spaceship. There are several different consoles with various screens, buttons, and switches. There is some clear signage in English throughout, indicating one side off stage being deeper into the ship and the other side leading to the door to outside.

On either the back wall or the fourth wall is a large screen/window showing the outside world. The ship is currently landed on an alien planet.

NOTES

* NOTE ON LANGUAGE

Throughout this play, many characters will speak using invented languages. Default to pronouncing these made-up words and sentences phonetically. There's no right or wrong pronunciation as long as the individual characters' pronunciations are consistent. After such lines, translations are provided in italics and brackets:

- STEPHEN. Mairi totorin gorspoo? *[What are you guys saying?]*

It's important that only the speakers comprehend what they are saying. The other characters shouldn't, and neither should the audience.

*NOTE ON TECH

This is a science fiction play, but the technological elements can be modified to fit the scale of your theater. They can be accomplished with practical effects, dramatic media, or sound design. For example, in the control room of the spaceship, there is a large screen displaying details and a view of the outside world. This could be accomplished with projections, screens, or simply placed on the fourth wall, invisible to the audience.

Similarly, there is a door to the outside world. A human-operated theatrical hydraulic door could be built, or it could simply be placed offstage and referred to through sound effects.

This play can be produced as elaborately or sparsely as need be. Strong sound design should buoy the atmosphere and environment.

"They should've sent a poet"
\- Carl Sagan, Contact

***

At rise, somewhere in the control room, Nora, a young woman in a mechanic's jumpsuit, messy hair pulled back, sits on the floor. She writes in a lovely bound notebook and mutters to herself.

NORA. And … with the last curve … of the orbit … around my neck. *(She pauses and reads it back in her head, then mutters a different phrase.)* From the pulse of gravity on my weary bones, I - *(The door to outside opens, and Stephen and Esther enter. They are both scientists, dressed in similar jumpsuits, but cleaner and fancier. They lug a large metal box. Nora sets her notebook down.)*

STEPHEN. And by the lake, we could put a library, the houses by the meadow.

ESTHER. Not our job! *(They set down the box.)* They have landscapers and architects to do all that. You focus on rocks, and I focus on nature. *(Stephen walks up to Esther. They get close and intimate.)*

STEPHEN. Like I'm not supposed to get carried away? The first humans on a habitable alien planet and I'm not allowed to fantasize about our future? *(They kiss. Esther cocks her head to indicate Nora.)*

STEPHEN. Nora, we've got the soil sample, flora samples, just getting the last few boxes of rocks, so let's get the ship ready to go.

NORA. On it.

ESTHER. Go get your rocks, rock boy. *(She kisses him on the check, and as he leaves, she slaps him on his butt.)*

NORA. Mary, begin Homeward Bound procedure.

MARY. *(Robotic voice V.O.)* Beginning Homeward Bound procedure. *(As Nora flips switches, checks dials, and presses buttons, Esther picks up the notebook Nora set down and flips through.)*

ESTHER. Now, what is this?

NORA. Put that down.

ESTHER. "Daydreams Past Jupiter?" I didn't know you were a writer.

NORA. You didn't know for a reason. Now give me back my poems!

ESTHER. Only if you share one.

NORA. It's bad luck to share a poem before it's finished. I've gotta make sure what's up here *(Points to head.)* matches what's down there. *(She points to notebook before snatching it from Esther and setting it down.)*

ESTHER. That's sweet, space mechanic poet. *(Nora shoots her a look.)* No, I mean, most of the ship techs we've worked with don't care for much beyond getting paid and getting from point A to point B.

NORA. Yeah. Poetry doesn't really pay the bills. And space gives me something worth writing about. *(Esther waits a beat to broach this subject.)*

ESTHER. You thought about coming back and starting the colony with us?

NORA. I belong on a ship, Esther. Not on land. Plus, I don't have the money to settle down.

ESTHER. We're about to get bonuses out the wazoo. The reward for finding a suitable planet for the colony is astronomical.

NORA. Then why don't all these little expeditions lie? Say we found paradise, get the bonus, and run?

ESTHER. We're scientists. We have integrity. *(Stephen screams from offstage. He sprints back onstage from off ship, clutching a bloody arm. He crumples on the floor.)*

STEPHEN. Shut the door, shut the door! *(Esther runs and hits a button. The door slams shut. There is a bang and scratching on the other side of the door.)*

STEPHEN. We need to go.

ESTHER. What happened?

NORA. What is that? *(Ferocious banging and scratching at the door.)*

STEPHEN. Launch the ship.

NORA. Mary, launch the ship!

MARY. Begin dual authentication.

NORA. Ship Op Authorization: Alpha Kilo Delta.

ESTHER. Lead Scientist Authorization: Lima, Mike, Echo. *(The ship shakes as the rockets launch them away from the planet.)*

MARY. Exiting atmosphere. *(Everyone lets out a breath. Esther crosses and kneels with Stephen.)*

ESTHER. What happened?

STEPHEN. Something bit me.

NORA. How? There are no animals on the planet.

STEPHEN. Guess they were hiding.

ESTHER. I'm just glad you're okay. *(They kiss.)* Nora, could you get a med pack? *(Nora exits to the back of the ship.)*

STEPHEN. It's fine. I just need to rest. *(He closes his eyes. Nora rushes back in and hands Esther the med pack. Esther begins to dress Stephen's wound.)*

NORA. Do we need to do something?

ESTHER. I'm trying.

NORA. No, I mean - do we need to tell someone? Call Earth? I mean, we should be following quarantine procedures. We shouldn't go home.

ESTHER. Nora, it's fine. Nothing got on the ship that wasn't supposed to. It's a bite, a wound, not cause for alarm.

NORA. I know that's not necessarily true -

ESTHER. How many medical supplies do we have back there?

NORA. …

ESTHER. Exactly. If we don't go back to Earth, we can't help Stephen. And that's if and only if there is something actually wrong. I'm the scientist, you're the mechanic. Stick to the ship.

NORA. Fine. It's your call. *(Stephen stirs and begins to wake up.)*

ESTHER. Hey baby. *(Stephen is utterly bewildered by this.)* Stephen?

STEPHEN. Alden? *[Esther?]*

NORA. What's Alden?

STEPHEN. *(Confusion escalates.)* Mairi totorin gorspoo? *[What are you guys saying?]*

NORA. Esther, why is he talking like that?

ESTHER. I don't know. *(Stephen moves towards Esther, but she and Nora move back.)*

STEPHEN. Mairizen dubtois tairee? *[What's happening to me?]*

NORA. Mary, what is he saying?

MARY. Nothing he says matches any patterns or languages in my records.

NORA. Maybe he's just lost his mind. Spewing gibberish. *(Stephen moves away from them to a sign on the wall. He studies it, confused.)*

ESTHER. Or somehow the bite damaged his language center … *(Stephen moves searches until he finds a writing utensil and something to write on. He writes, then shows it to Nora and Esther. On it is a written language, similar to one we might know, but unintelligible.)*

NORA. These are words, sentences. Like he forgot English and is trying to speak in some other tongue. *(Frustrated at their not understanding, Stephen sits down at a console, and writes away.)*

ESTHER. Mary, can you recognize anything in this? *(She holds up the note to a sensor.)*

MARY. No recognizable pattern, but with further written and spoken samples, we might be able to begin to construct a cipher to communicate.

NORA. Maybe that's what Stephen's doing now. *(She gestures over.)* He's writing, scribbling. Maybe he'll come up with something useful.

ESTHER. Nora, could you say that again? I couldn't quite hear you.

NORA. Just that maybe Stephen will come up with something useful. *(Esther steps back from Nora.)*

ESTHER. Are you sure you're feeling alright? You - you keep slurring your words.

NORA. I'm not slurring my words.

ESTHER. You just did it again!

NORA. Mary, run speech analysis. Am I slurring my words?

MARY. Speech analysis complete. No misarticulation detected.

ESTHER. Why does she sound like that?

NORA. Esther, maybe you need to sit down.

ESTHER. Why does her voice sound pletuch *[low]* like that?

NORA. Esther, sit down.

ESTHER. I don't blauck drugan spree *[feel so good]*. *(Blood begins to trickle out of Esther's ear.)*

NORA. It's going to be okay.

ESTHER. Nora, I think it got you. Whatever infected Stephen. I can't understand half of what you or Mary are saying. You must be sick, too.

NORA. I understand Mary perfectly.

ESTHER. No. No. Catowken. Catowken *[Can't be. Can't be]*. Wait! Stephen might glaurden stochren *[understand me]*. Stephen. Stephen! *(Esther runs over to where Stephen continues to write. She spins him around, grabs his arms, and talks right in his face.)* Drau, Klaus stochren glaurden catow percanow. Drau! *[Stephen, please tell me you can hear. Stephen!]*

STEPHEN. *(Bewildered; shakes off her grip.)* Troi notkai *[You're hurting me]*.

ESTHER. *(To Nora.)* Drau catowken glaurden. Persnout acroo. *[Stephen can't understand. He's confused as before]* Tot! Tot! *[No! No!]* *(Esther gives up on verbal communication and instead shakes her head to indicate no and points emphatically at Stephen. She lets out a cry of anguish then keels over in stomach pain.)*

NORA. Esther – *(She goes down to help her, but Esther rises and coughs up blood, spraying Nora in the face.)*

ESTHER. Navostay. Navostay *[Alone. Alone.]* *(Esther runs offstage, deeper in the ship. Nora wipes her face.)*

NORA. Mary, please tell me you recognize what Esther was saying.

MARY. It does not match any of the recorded languages in my database or any linguistic patterns -

NORA. Then what are you good for?

MARY. It also doesn't match any of Stephen's speech.

NORA. You said we could make a cipher to understand Stephen. Could we make one for Esther, too?

MARY. We could, but it would be harder. With each added new language, potential communication and understanding becomes exponentially more difficult.

NORA. You say that like you think this is going to keep happening.

MARY. There's no evidence to suggest Stephen's affliction won't keep spreading.

NORA. How could it? Language isn't contagious.

MARY. Possible methods of contamination include touch, exchange of bodily liquids, water vapor, or proximity. *(Nora moves away from Stephen.)*

NORA. Mary, what is the likelihood I am already infected?

MARY. … There is a 98% certainty that you are either already infected or will be infected before you leave.

NORA. Mary, I need you to tell me. What happens if it keeps spreading? How much time would we have.

MARY. … I don't think I should answer that question.

NORA. I'm not … I just need to know.

MARY. It could take as long as three years for everyone on Earth to become infected.

NORA. And as little as?

MARY. … As little as eighteen hours. *(Nora thinks for a moment, but then begins flipping a few switches, typing inputs on a screen.)*

NORA. We can't bring this back. This can't reach Earth. We need to land on some deserted planet or stop in orbit or crash or -

MARY. I cannot alter my flight path without the approval of at least two crew members.

NORA. They're clearly incapacitated.

MARY. I cannot ignore my programming.

NORA. There has to be a way around.

MARY. This could be accomplished with a full system reset through hard drive key.

NORA. Where's the key?

MARY. The Lead Scientist was instructed to put it somewhere safe. *(Nora begins to search through the control room for the key. It starts hurriedly but quickly escalates to panickily tearing through the room. It gets the attention of Stephen, who stops writing and turns. Esther reenters from the back of the ship and watches, confused. She looks around the control room. She recognizes some of the switches that are flipped and realizes.)*

ESTHER. Cevastapoul letchye snaur. *[You're trying to kill us all]. (She looks, sees where Nora is searching and dashes past her. She sorts around some boxes and finds a small lockbox. She opens it and pulls out a small key. She holds it up and coughs or stomps to get Nora's attention.)*

NORA. Mary, is that the hard drive key?

MARY. Affirmative.

NORA. Esther, I need you to hand me that key.

ESTHER. Praudo slee? *[Want this?]*

NORA. Esther, I really need you to hand me that key. *(Nora reaches out her arm and slowly steps forward. Esther puts the key in her mouth and swallows.)*

NORA. No! *(She rushes at Esther and tries to pry her mouth open. Stephen runs and pulls Nora away. Esther proudly opens her mouth and sticks out her tongue. The key is gone.)*

NORA. You selfish bitch. *(Esther puts her hand up to her ear and shrugs, miming out that she can't understand her. Nora fights against Stephen's grip, but he does not yield.)*

STEPHEN. Naurdeen snaogli pertan. *[Shouldn't have attacked my wife].*

NORA. Mary, you can't let anyone on this ship, you hear me?

MARY. I'm afraid that will be out of my control. *(Nora*

weighs the hopelessness of the situation in front of her. She kicks Stephen and pushes him off her. She rushes to a control console and kicks it. She rips off a panel and begins to tear out cables.)

ESTHER. Nauri! *[Hey!] (She runs up to Nora and tries to stop her. Nora shoves her. Hard. Stephen grabs his writing utensil and stabs Nora in the back. She roars, swings, and wails on Stephen with her fists until he crumples. She walks over to another console and flips switches and hits buttons seemingly at random.)*

MARY. *(Lower cadence than before.)* Nora, I must ask you to stop before you stourlyn gern zhoule *[destroy my systems]. (Nora stops.)*

NORA. What did you say, Mary?

MARY. Sniezi perlin tine sliiv. *[You are jeopardizing this ship]. (Nora realizes what this means. Terror begins to grab at her just as Esther rises behind her. Esther grabs a sheet of metal and slams it right onto Nora's head.)*

Blackout.

END OF PLAY

BOOK'D

by Rachel Keown

Three women lounge at a Bed & Breakfast, enjoying wine and cheese hour. One recently got a bad review about her driftwood art. One has pizza waiting in the car that she was supposed to bring home to her husband. And the other was recently arrested for disrupting her own wedding reception. And now, it's time to unwind and maybe talk about books. (Comedy, 1M, 3W)

CHARACTERS

SHELLEY
Female/female-presenting, Gen Z-adjacent; Artisan.

HYLIE
Female, 30s-40s; Reasonable.

GINA
Female, Older than the other two; From somewhere in the South.

GINA'S HUSBAND
Male; A disembodied voice via speakerphone.

SETTING

The top deck of the Halcyon House Bed & Breakfast; Outer Banks, North Carolina. 1:40pm

***

Waves push in the tide and join the sound of occasional rolls of thunder; a storm brews in The Outer Banks.

Closer still, sits the top porch of the Halcyon House Bed & Breakfast. White-washed shiplap floorboards broken in over time by Old World Money.

Three women lounge in Adirondack chairs. A table with refreshments rests near their feet. The Halcyon House hosts a daily, complimentary wine and cheese hour from 1-2pm.

A number of empty wine bottles scatter among the women. The time is 1:40. Gravity is an issue.

SHELLEY. One negative article. One. By some Buzzfeed troll.

HYLIE. You don't think he understood your art?

SHELLEY. Driftwood is a misunderstood artistic medium-

GINA. *(Decants a red wine.)* What's to understand? No one wants driftwood tchotchkes stinking up their home, smelling like "fish carcass, wood rot, and Jesus Christ-Did-Somebody-Shit-On-My-Couch." Meanwhile, you're trying to compete with the authority on beach-scented para-phernalia; Bath & Body Works' figured out heaven in a hand soap with "Endless Sea." Discontinued now, bless its heart.

SHELLEY. --I clean it, you monster--

GINA. --Did you know--I recently learned--you should hold a flashlight underneath red wine to make sure you aren't drinking sediment. Older wines tend to carry par-ti-cu-lates--

SHELLEY. *(To Hylie.)* --I don't use just any driftwood that comes floating along. I specifically use pieces from the Outer Banks. The home of The Lost Colony. The place where people inexplicably-and-mystically-disappeared. Then, I elevate these wooden time capsules, these ancestors of the mysteriously carved tree that befuddled a colony; and an entire continent, even.

GINA. We understand it just fine. Now listen: I'm over here trying to talk about drinking sediment and no one seems to care - *(Hylie inspects an empty bottle.)*

HYLIE. This is Aldi's store brand wine. "Winking Owl. 2021." I don't know anything about particulates, but the presence of actual grapes seems dubious. *(She sets the bottle down and constructs a cheese cube tower.)*

GINA. *(Mutters.)* --ya'll're unrefined as hell. *(She removes her phone from her purse, clicks on the flashlight, then accosts the bottom of a wine bottle. Probably white.)* Ope! Well this one ain't even red! But I wonder-- *(Examines anyway, hushed.)* --ohhyep. I chipped off lotsa cork in there--

HYLIE. Yum.

SHELLEY. *(Still in story-mode.)* --some of my pieces are people-sized. I've made chandeliers, coffee tables--

HYLIE. --uh-huh. Yeah, no, I understand. What. You. Are. Saying--

SHELLEY. *(Worked up.)* But the art of it--like, you don't even know--

GINA. *(To Hylie.)* --I guess you don't know--

HYLIE. --I must not know--

SHELLEY. --How could you know, it's a "misunderstood medium." By design--

HYLIE. --ahhh, I definitely understand. Eclecticism breeds interest, right--?

SHELLEY. *(Beat.)* Who do you think you are? Some art authority? Some art critic, criticizing my work? You look me in the eye when you say that ... *(Gina's flashlight spotlights Shelley face; Shelley shields her eyes in agony. The flashlight remains "ON" for the rest of the play.)*

GINA. Proper wine etiquette dictates that you pour from left to right. Should we do that? *(She regains authority over the phone. Gina strugglepours: center, right, left...)* That was deceptively difficult. Sommelier I am not.

SHELLEY. My art is about surrendering our sadness-es

into the unknown--

GINA. *(Dissociates, wistful.)* --that's impossible; it ceaselessly drifts inland. It's not surrendering sadness, it's joining it. Closer and closer until the salty waves of isolation pull us into the sea and drown us in the abyss of loneliness. The discontinued Bath & Body Works hand soap understood. An "Endless Sea..." *(Bright.)* --Im'ma try and get a group photo right quick.

SHELLEY. --You have this thing in your hands that's gone on a journey, traveled thousands of miles—including shipping-- *(Gina squeezes herself between Hylie and Shelley, fidgets with the phone's screen.)*

GINA. *(Together.)* --We got an eyeball--
HYLIE. *(Together.)* --It makes sense now. Driftwood, wood that drifts--

SHELLEY. THAT--YES. *(Pause.)* THERE IT IS--THAT IS EXACTLY MY POINT, you took the words out of my mouth--it's rebirth. The new mother to land creatures when it banks. It's beautiful--

GINA. --the tiny little Nemos--

SHELLEY. I take it, I make--no. No! Nemo would die on land, and who would find Nemo then? Seagulls. And they'd eat him. That is some bougie circle of life shit right there-- and that's the wrong movie, Gina. I take it and make magic with it.

HYLIE. And money--

SHELLEY. *(Tearful.)* -- "the ciiiircle of liiiife..." *(Gina imposes a group photo upon everyone. She returns to her chair, scrolls through her phone.*

GINA. *(To herself.)* Shoot--it did that rapid-photo thing. I got 14 photos of Shelley's eyeball-- *(To Shelley.)* Shelley, you photograph "lazy-eyed." Anyone ever told you, you have a lazy eye? Turn your head this way next time. Oh, there's one, okay, I think we got a good one in here. Shelley:

next time turn your head this way. *(She demonstrates whatever that is.)*

SHELLEY. --but then: Buzzfeed happened! Which I don't think it's the most viable judge of commerce. This troll's article "re"- "por"- "ted" on his Wiccan ex-girlfriend putting a spell on him because he said the wand he bought from me actually had magical properties, even though my website clearly states in a small disclaimer at the bottom of the ordering page, "I don't make magic, but the ocean gifts me treasures--"

HYLIE. --That sounds extremely magical. On a scale of Muggle to Magical: it sounds Magical times 1000--

SHELLEY. --He said that she "spelled him into an incel." But she said he'd cheated on her so "it was justified." It cascaded into thousands of comments, people chiming in with their "medical degrees" they got from Google.com University; High Priests of Wiccan covens offering reverse spells, love spells, binding spells. Folks lost their minds over "The Phallus of Horror." That was the title of the article, I loved the title of the article. But I thought I was fucked.

HYLIE. But you weren't--

SHELLEY. --No. In fact, the title gave me the idea for the business I have now. Hand-crafted, polished driftwood dildos. Talk about an unsaturated market. $200-1000 a dick; even more if customized. I'm one of Forbes' "30 Under 30." I just launched satellite stores in Italy, Amsterdam. "Ride the Tide" is international.

HYLIE. That's exactly what women need. A wooden injection that makes their cooch smell like the ocean.

GINA. --Well. Hoo-ray for cock-- *(Hylie pours herself another glass of wine.)*

HYLIE. *(Downs glass.)* --Another "30 Under 30--" *(Gina places a cheese tray on her lap.)*

GINA. Should probably put something besides wine in our stomachs now. *(Shelley refills everyone's glasses with Aldi chardonnay anyway. Gina reads off a card from the tray.)* "Extra sharp cheddar, Tillamook Or-eee-gone." Oh, now I didn't know Or-eee-gone was known for their cheeses.

SHELLEY. That's white-noise cheese.

GINA. *(Moves on, reads.)* "Baby Swiss, Arden Hills, Minnesota."

SHELLEY. Land-O-Lakes! They're repurposing junk, trying to pawn it off as something special--

HYLIE. --imagine that--

GINA. You'll eat it and like it. Oh ... listen to this one, listen to--it has an actual name: *(Reads.)* "Cornelia. Corneeeel-eee-uh. Point 'Reese,' California." Cornelia cheese, from Land-O-Reese's--

SHELLEY. Point Reyes. "King's Point," actually, but whatever, not everyone speaks casual Spanish--

GINA. --listen to me. Flexing my "affineur" muscle today-

HYLIE. *(Eyes sear into Shelley.)* --someone's flexing their casual asshole muscle--

GINA. Kegel. Very effective. *(Card.)* This is also the only cheese that came with a description, listen here: *(Reads.)* "Pasteurized cow's milk, creamy, bright flavor." This is the one right here, ladies. This is the--first up. *(They spread the Cornelia across crackers-- Hylie and Shelley, a reasonable amount; Gina slathers it. They bite in unison ... a moment of silence.)*

GINA. It's not bright ... so much as it is ... oppressively pungent--

HYLIE. I'm not an effen-hour here, but that wasn't a description so much as a warning--

GINA. I'm getting a real backdrop of toes. Anyone else-- are ya'll getting that? *(Despite herself, Gina swallows the toe-cheese. A dark cloud descends upon her sunny disposition.)*

SHELLEY. What is happening to her--

HYLIE. She ate too much, man. Too much! That stuff was so bad it destroyed all the good stuff inside her ...

SHELLEY. We're witnessing the rise of a cheese phoenix-

GINA. About six months ago my husband was moving boxes up from the basement and he smashed his foot on the stairs. When he made a second trip up, damned if he didn't do it again, same spot, same foot. Well, over time, his big toenail began to, kind-of, separate. They call this a "subungual hematoma." I have one of those degrees from Google.com University too, but with a minor in WebMD. Flash forward a piece, it's worse, and there is now a whole n'other one growing all up under the first one, like two toenails stacked in a deck of cards--we say that in our house now when things are too close together, "Like two toenails stacked in a deck of cards." So these sons of bitches are causing him a lot of pain and whatnot, and I keep telling him he needs to see a philanderer-

SHELLEY. --podiatrist--

GINA. –"podi-a-trician," but he doesn't feel that it's necessary, " It'll resolve itself. Maybe a year or so." A year or--! He starts wearing this weird little silicone tube over it, 'cause the dog kept stepping on it, and damnit if the dog's pointy little macaroni nails didn't end up right in that decaying toe cuticle every single time--

HYLIE. --aw, noooo. Those are the Legos of feet--

GINA. --So, but, the other night when we were having our "shush-the-bad-the-put-the-bible-in-the-side-tabledrawer" times; that toe sleeve slid right off and ya'll. You. All. Ohmygod. This. Right here. *(She rages against the Cornelia. Hylie and Shelley take a seat for Gina's sermon. Or take cover, whichever.)* But it's not just that. *(Downs a hefty glass of wine.)* It's the continuous fart-u-lations. The beard hairs on my granite double vanity. The Funyon shards scraping m'legs in my Egypt cotton bedsheets. Imma tell you, when I walk into the kitchen and see his plate sitting in the sink, right next to an empty dishwasher ... Jesus take the wheel, Lorena Bobbitt hold me back. Let me ask you something: how does one man go through five forks in a single day? He's never sittin' down to no Pretty-Woman-Julia-Roberts shrimp fork, salad fork, dessert fork, I-have-to-count-the-fork-tines-fork meal. Now look here: All I've asked him for, all I've ever wanted is to go on a vacation to the Outer Banks, buy some defective kites at Kitty Hawk for our friends, and spend the rest of my time away from a hotbox of fartin', decayin' body parts. I want to go to a spa and have little live fish baits eatin' the dead skin off m'feet while women slather my face with mud and salad, and drink champagne infused with gold and, I don't know, flecks of hundred dollar bills, and bubbles made from the tears of moderately-comfortable upper-middle-class women who cry because no matter how fast they speed walk in their Sketchers their milkshakes are never going to bring the boys to their yard, their neighbor's yard, or any yard because it was never approved by the Homeowner's Association. But I had to keep all this to myself. It was hard enough to earn this vacation. So in conclusion, I don't know how I'm going to discreetly pay off the $2000 charge for the spa treatment I blackout-rage booked this morning.

SHELLEY. *(Beat.)* I wasn't going to say anything, but your skin is so dry I bet I could sand wood on your cheeks--

HYLIE. --It's like I'm talking to an oily paper birch--

SHELLEY. --I haven't been able to stop staring at your eye bags--

HYLIE. --They're more like overstuffed luggage--

SHELLEY. --For the love of God, don't cancel the spa

appointment-- *(Gina shines the camera flashlight under her own chin. Hylie and Shelley stumble backward at the grotesque gesture; they take cover for certain.)*

GINA. *(Makes some kind of face.)* --this was me an hour ago. *(Moves flashlight into hero pose.)* This is me now: The Cheese Phoenix. *(She demonstrates ... that.)*

HYLIE. *(To Shelley.)* Maybe you and I didn't eat enough of the Cornelia ...

GINA. *(In a "different realm".)* --Phoenix. No. I'm not a Phoenix; do you know who I remind myself of?

SHELLEY. There's no possible way to know--

HYLIE. --No, I think I know--

GINA. HAVE YOU'UN'S SEEN "JOKER?"

HYLIE. *(Together.)* --Yes, it's a surrealist masterpiece--
SHELLEY. *(Together.)* --It's a misogynistic pat on the back--

GINA. *(As Joaquin Phoenix as "Arthur Fleck")* "You know what's really funny? You know what really makes me laugh? I used to think my life was a tragedy. Now I realize ... it's a fuckin' comedy." *(Produces pack of cigarettes from nowhere.)* I keep these in my purse for emergencies. Emergency use ONLY. And for all the time. *(They all drink.)* There's this part in "Joker" where Arthur Fleck, he's just killed this guy, just annihilated him with this pair of scissors--spoiler alert, Shelley--

SHELLEY. --I said I've seen it--

GINA. --and then he's on these stairs in the Bronx--

HYLIE. Interesting aside, the people who lived near those stairs in the Bronx at the time of filming became pissed off because of the Instagram traffic it brought along with it. They were all like, "Get off my lawn, you Gen Z Influencer Generation of Trash Fires!" No offense, Shelley--

SHELLEY. I'm not Gen Z. I'm Assimilated.

GINA. --Arthur's just killed this guy-- *(Lights cigarette, imitates Arthur's dance movements.)* He's had this moment of acceptance that he is who he is, and he's almost fully Jokered up, he's walking down the hall of his apartment, he's all swagger in his signature suit--he ends up on these Bronx stairs dancing this jazzy dance. And the music in the background is that one song … *(Gary Glitter's "Rock and Roll Part 2")* "Doooo do doooo do dooooooo: do do dooooo do doooooo do doooooo--"

SHELLEY. Gary Glitter's "Rock and Roll Part 2."

GINA. Okay, sure--

HYLIE. THAT'S the name of that song?! That's the stupidest fuckin' name I've ever--WOOOW--

GINA. He's on this high. He's transformed his face--he's seen the light-- *(She mounts an Adirondack chair, shifts the flashlight above her head higher, the cigarette smoke curls above her.)*

HYLIE. SERIOUSLY! One of the most commonly used songs in goddamn movies and commercials? Rock and Roll. Part. Two. That can't-- *(Pulls out phone, searches.)* "Rock and Roll Part 2." *(Plays song, continues search.)* That would indicate, then, that there is a "Rock and Roll Part 1" …

GINA. *(Moves, speaks in slow-motion.)* He moves in slow-motion ... *("Rock and Roll Part 2" does not stop. Gina abandons her phone at some point. Grabs a wad of Cornelia.)*

HYLIE. Indeed, there is a Part One. And, OH! And the singer was a convicted sex offender--that's just, that's goddamn unfortunate--

GINA. "I am an agent of chaos. Introduce a little anarchy."

HYLIE. That's Heath Ledger's Joker.

GINA. "You ever dance with the devil in the pale

moonlight?"

SHELLEY. That's, well, that's obviously Jack Nicholson--

GINA. "YOU CAN'T HANDLE THE TRUTH!"

SHELLEY. No--

HYLIE. --Not even close. But, Gina, this is your vacation. *(Squares Gina's shoulders.)* You've got nothing left to lose; who gives two shits about the spa bill. You didn't "earn" the spa, and you weren't "owed" it. YOU OWN IT. It's yours. You're going to go back to that spa, get all that dead skin eaten off by tiny fish, and go get your own muddy clown face because--

GINA. *(Mimics iconic "leg kick" from Joker-stair dance in the Adirondack chair)* I get what I FUCKIN' DESERVE! *(Spikes the Cornelia.)* "Behold! The power of cheese--" AGHSHIT! Oh, sweet Jesus!! *(Cigarette ash drops onto Gina's face and she falls sideways into the chairs, the table, the cheese; Gina is an agent of chaos.)*

SHELLEY. *(Together.)* --What happened?!

HYLIE. *(Together.)* --What's wrong!!

GINA. ASH IN MY EYEBALL. How did he do it--green screen/CGI or something--NO ONE can smoke a cigarette and dance at the same time! Lord, the Spirit of Joaquin was not with me to-day! *(The lit cigarette has disappeared. Gina tries to get her bearings but grabs a chair at the wrong angle and it flips over. Hylie attempts to catch her, her foot slips on the spiked Cornelia--they make a two-person-Adirondackchair sandwich.)*

SHELLEY. Man down! We got a man--

HYLIE. Like two toenails stacked in a deck of cards.

SHELLEY. Bitch's toe-up. *(Gina stands. She has adopted the Adirondack chair as a pseudo-turtle shell. Hylie rises; she and Shelley aim cheese cubes at the back of Gina's chair in a makeshift game of cornhole.)*

GINA. If I carry it, I can't trip backwards on it. If I carry--it can't--I won't fall. *(She hunch-teeters on one leg in a near-fall. Her phone rings; she toddles to answer it on speakerphone.)*

GINA'S HUSBAND. Gina?

GINA. This is Gina.

GINA'S HUSBAND. Did you get lost on the way from getting the pizza?

SHELLEY. *(Stops throwing cheese.)* Wait, what?

HYLIE. Like one of the artisan pizza places here? A place that also serves fresh catch that comes right out of the ocean in the morning, right--?

GINA. --he hates sea food. It's Little Caesars. *(Mutes phone, to others.)* --something smells like burning, do, ya'll smell that? *(Unmutes.)* I made a stop along the way. I was ... "window shopping" earlier and I saw this flier for a book club that took place during a wine-and-cheese-and-wine hour, so I decided to join.

GINA'S HUSBAND. What book? What are you talking about? We're on vacation, you don't read on vacations--

GINA. --I'll be there shortly. *(A cheese cube bounces off the back of Gina's head. Hylie recovers an unopened bottle of wine from the floor, opens, pours three glasses, one of them all the way to the brim. She places it under Gina's face; she drinks horizontally.)*

GINA'S HUSBAND. You're eating without me?

SHELLEY. *(Sniffs the air.)* Wait, I smell it too ...

HYLIE. Is it something salty with a strong backdrop of bitter condescension?

GINA'S HUSBAND. Who's that?

GINA. Girls, 's little callous. *(A fire sprouts in a bag behind them. Hylie turns, leaps toward the bag.)*

HYLIE. Oh, my GOD! OH, my god! *(Looks closer.)* Your

Joaquin cigarette is burning up my Jansport! It's the fanciest thing I own.

GINA. *(Into phone.)* Herbie, I gotta go! I started another fire--

GINA'S HUSBAND. Gina?! GINA?! The pizza--

GINA. Be there later, bye-- *(Positions herself in front of the bag.)* Stand back! Stand back--I know what to do--! *(She takes a deep breath, stands up straight, prepares for the world's most epic, sacrificial trust fall.)*

SHELLEY. She doesn't know what she's doing--!

HYLIE. Did she say, "Another fire...??!"

GINA. I always knew I was gonna go out this way... ! *(She tips backward. The Adirondack chair lands safely on all fours above the burning backpack.)*

HYLIE. *(Beat.)* What did that do?

GINA. Imma be honest, my back was hurtin' and I needed to sit down. But I thought the wind trajectory or the gale force of my sittin' would just, whooosh the fire into extinguishment.

HYLIE. It didn't!

GINA. *(Jumps up.)* I realize that.

HYLIE. Put it out, PUT IT OUT!

SHELLEY. I got it—*(She whisks over to the scene with an open bottle of Winking Owl, ready to douse the fire--Hylie shoves her and her Keystone Cop of an idea back from whence it came. Hylie removes her flip-flop and bats the fire down with the force of an entire Controlled Burn team. She picks apart remnants of her bag: Disconnected straps, a charred wallet, a singed book.)*

GINA. Oh! Look there. The book we was supposed to be discussing.

HYLIE. Yes.

GINA. I was excited when I saw the flier at the bookstore downtown. My original plans today with my husband included hang gliding in Kill Devil Hills. I feel like the name might've foreshadowed the day's outcome. I almost bought the book, but its dustjacket wasn't going to match the aesthetic of my living room back home, so I just showed up for the wine and cheese. What'd you call this book club outfit, the name was too cute. Book Time, Booky-Book-Book, Book-It--

SHELLEY. Ohhhhh! Book-iiiiiit! I loved those free personal pan pizzas in grade school! Though, my disdain for reading is a direct result of knowing I won't be rewarded with pizza.

HYLIE. Why are you here?

SHELLEY. I live here in Manteo. I come for the free wine and cheese hour almost every day.

HYLIE. Didn't even read the book--

SHELLEY. I didn't even read the flier you apparently posted. What kind of psycho invites strangers to hang out and discuss a book? Who reads on vacation--you don't read on vacations. The only thing I've read in years is the Buzzfeed article. Followed by a quiz to determine what flavor of ice cream I'd be--

HYLIE. --I'm happy for you, knowing that you've made millions without reading an actual book--

GINA. --BOOK'D! How'd you come up with the name?

HYLIE. *(Beat.)* Came to me the other night in a holding cell waiting to post bail. *(Shelley bursts into laughter. Gina examines Hylie's flipflop-fire-extinguisher, sniffs it, sits at death's door--)*

GINA. *(Re: her stinky discovery.)* --What in god's name is this--uuugggghhhh--

SHELLEY. But, no, for real.

HYLIE. --A week ago I had my wedding reception here. I found the man I'd just exchanged vows within our Bridal Suite with I-Still-Don't-Even-Know-Who. I'd had a few, decked the woman in the mouth ... I might've found my way down to the beach and started destroying the snow fences with-- *(Pours wine, toasts Shelley.)* --a big piece of driftwood. Cops picked me up and I spent the night in jail. I found this book in the back of the toilet in a Ziplock. Wondered if anyone around here found this as useful as I did.

SHELLEY. But why are you still at the B&B?

HYLIE. We were gifted two weeks here. I wasn't going to let it go to waste. I also had a lot of gifts to open. Lotta cards. I made a small fortune. Need two grand, Gina? T ake what you need. *(She removes a soot-covered Ziplock bag of cash, tosses it to Gina.)*

GINA. Did you repurpose the toilet Ziplock--? *(Hylie pours whatever wine remains.)* --You know, the pizza's just been sitting in my car ... in the sun ... *(Peels Cornelia off Hylie's flip-flop.)* It'll be fine--

SHELLEY. What was the toilet literature?

HYLIE. <u>The Subtle Art of Not Giving a Fuck.</u>

END OF PLAY

FAITH

By Christine Hsu

A chaplain interning at a hospital chapel consults her first patient – a teenage boy. As they connect, she realizes that she has just as much to learn from him as he does her. (Drama, 1M, 1W)

CHARACTERS

DEAN
Male, 15; non-white.

GRACE
Female, 25

SETTING

A dimly lit chapel within a hospital ward with pews. Stained glass windows and a giant wooden cross are in the very back.

***

At rise, Grace enters. She faces the audience and does the sign of the cross. She doesn't notice Dean is sitting in the very back right stage pew. Grace facing the audience, smiles and sits on the front row pew to the left side.

DEAN. Dude - you're the first person I've ever seen come in here!

GRACE. *(Turns.)* Oh - I didn't see you there. *(Dean walks up to her and decides to sit on a pew in the front row, but on stage right.)*

DEAN. Yup - I kinda blend in.

GRACE. I didn't mean to disturb you.

DEAN. No, it's fine. I just like the peace and quiet here.

GRACE. My name is Grace. Chaplain Grace. Well, chaplain in training. *(She sticks out her hand. Apprehensive, Dean looks at her hand, then slowly walks over and shakes her hand, then walks back to the pew he was sitting at.)*

DEAN. Hmm - it's nice to meet you. My name is Dean.

GRACE. This is my first day.

DEAN. To chaplain?

GRACE. Sort of - I'm interning here, while I go to seminary school.

DEAN. Never met a female priest.

GRACE. Oh no - I'm Lutheran, not Catholic - I'm a pastor.

DEAN. My bad. They let women be pastors?

GRACE. They have only been doing it since 2000. I'm under the Lutheran Evangelical Protestant Church.

DEAN. Evangelical, yikes.

GRACE. No, no, no - we're the most progressive of the Lutherans.

DEAN. Sure. *(He fiddles with his hands.)* So what type of advice are you giving.

GRACE. *(She smiles and brings out a bible with multiple colored tabs.)* Spiritual guidance. I've got this. Quiz away.

DEAN. A man loses his wife.

GRACE. *(She flips to a passage and reads.)* Matthew 5:4 - Blessed are those who mourn, for they will be comforted.

DEAN. How about dealing with a grandparent with dementia?

GRACE. *(She flips to another passage. Not the right one. Flips to another passage and reads.)* John 15:12-13 - My command is this: Love each other as I have loved you. Greater love has no one than this: to lay down one's life for one's friends.

DEAN. Cancer.

GRACE. *(She flips to another passage and reads.)* Exodus 14:14 - The Lord will fight for you; you need only to be still.

DEAN. How about if you've been still and don't believe in the Lord? How about if you're 15 and the chemo isn't working and your mom and dad are crying in the waiting room?

GRACE. Oh God - I'm so sorry. Shit - I didn't mean to be so blase about helping people.

DEAN. Nah - it was funny to see you flip through your book of answers.

GRACE. Gosh - I probably shouldn't curse either with patients and parishioners. Working on it. I'm an intern. Chaplain in training, NOT a full chaplain.

DEAN. Gotcha *(Pause.)* Must be nice to believe in a God. Can't really believe in Jesus. *(He points up towards the audience near the lighting.)* I don't really look like him.

GRACE. I don't look like him either.

DEAN. How can you relate to him or a higher being? Some white dude with a white beard and white robes.

GRACE. I don't know if it's a white guy up there - but a higher being that looks like a composite of us.

DEAN. So the most woke God out there.

GRACE. Maybe. My dad is a scientist, but a lifelong Christian. For him, heaven is being in the presence of God and hell is the absence of God.

DEAN. Deep, but how about if you just don't know what to believe in?

GRACE. Wait - I've got something. *(She flips through the bible again and points at a page.)* Psalms 46:1-3 - God is our refuge and strength, an ever-present help in trouble. Therefore we will not fear, though the earth gives way and the mountains fall into the heart of the sea, though its waters roar and foam and the mountains quake with their surging.

DEAN. Pretty passage. Don't you ever question the existence of God?

GRACE. Of course, all the time. But when you question, you build your faith.

DEAN. I was never raised anything, but my cousin Sue is SUPER Christian. I remember driving with my mom, sister - Rachel, Aunt Mary and Sue to the Grand Canyon. My cousin Sue looked out the window and told me - look. What are you talking about? I asked her. There it is - the God Shot. What? I looked out and the sky was violet, grey, tangerine, periwinkle and a dozen other colors. Sue explained to me - when you see a sunset like that - how can you not believe in a God?

GRACE. She has a point.

DEAN. Yeah, I guess, but not really. I don't know. I can't seem to figure out why I have cancer and other assholes don't.

GRACE. Hmm …

DEAN. I mean, I didn't rape or kill anyone. Okay, I've definitely stolen Halloween candy from my kid sister, but I'm not a total dick.

GRACE. That's rough.

DEAN. Ugh - I don't want to face Aunt Mary and Sue, if they are out there comforting my mom.

GRACE. Hiding out from them in here.

DEAN. Yup - when we did the road trip, we stopped at the Rothko Chapel. Been?

GRACE. No.

DEAN. It's in Houston, Texas. You walk in and there are Bibles, Korans and Torahs to flip through. You'd be home with your book of answers. Inside the chapel are these HUGE dark purple paintings and light coming in from the ceiling and a bunch of benches. Instead of being contemplative, it's more dire and desperate.

GRACE. Did you know you had cancer when you went on the trip?

DEAN. Yeah - I didn't really want to go - but then again - it would make my family happy.

GRACE. Make-A-Wish?

DEAN. Nah - I don't really need to go to Disney World. I puked after going on the Cyclone when I was a kid.

GRACE. Anything you really want?

DEAN. Dunno - to stay alive, but that's not in the cards for me.

GRACE. Wait. *(She flips to another page in the bible.)* Ecclesiastes 3:2 - A time to be born, and a time to die; a time to plant, and a time to pluck up what is planted.

DEAN. My dad did tell me that the day you are born into the world is the first day you start dying.

GRACE. He's right about that.

DEAN. His name is Matthew. Can you read me that first passage again?

GRACE. *(Flips back to the first passage.)* Blessed are those who mourn, for they will be comforted.

DEAN. *(Quietly repeats.)* Blessed are those who mourn, for they will be comforted. *(Gets up and sits next to Grace.)* Let me see that book of answers.

GRACE. *(She hands Dean the book.)* It's not a book of answers, but more of a book of spiritual guidance. *(Dean flips through the book and laughs. Hands the book back to Grace.)*

DEAN. Gosh - there are like 100 Post-its. I think you went overboard.

GRACE. I'm trying to be a good student and yes - went a

little overboard. *(She shoves the book into her purse.)*

DEAN. It's nice to talk to you. I may not believe in all the stuff you believe, but it's nice to talk to someone that doesn't know me.

GRACE. Sure, here to help?

DEAN. Psalm 30-5 - Weeping may tarry for the night, but joy comes with the morning.

GRACE. You read the bible?

DEAN. Nah - but it's my cousin Sue's favorite passage. She always wakes up early to run cross country. Either sunrise or sunset, and she's there.

GRACE. I hate running.

DEAN. Me too. *(He gets up and paces back and forth, and then stops and looks at Grace.)* I don't know what the fuck I'm doing with dying. I mean, we were doing the chemo, but ultimately it's not working. I just think random shit like, I was suppose to learn how to drive next year or I've never going to have sex or will all my high school friends just forget about me when I graduate and be done with it.

GRACE. That's an understandable feeling.

DEAN. Yeah … *(He sits back down in his original spot.)*

GRACE. I don't know much about death, but I know it's tough. I've only been to my grandpa's funeral.

DEAN. What was that like?

GRACE. Overwhelming. I was a little kid and these random old folks kept sobbing and hugging me and telling me about how great my grandpa was. I remember going up to the casket and he was white as a ghost with make-up on. It didn't seem real. I wanted to cry but couldn't.

DEAN. I don't know if I want a bunch of folks sobbing at my funeral.

GRACE. I take solace in the fact my best friend already wrote my eulogy.

DEAN. Let's hear it. *(Grace pulls up her smartphone and scrolls to a passage.)*

GRACE. Grace liked cats. Pause. Grace liked guys. Pause. Grace liked guys that have cats. Pause. Grace liked guys that have cats but are dicks. Pause. The end.

DEAN. Whoa, your life is kinda lame.

GRACE. No shit. I'm on Tinder - I'll find a guy eventually with a nice cat.

DEAN. You hook up on Tinder as a priest?

GRACE. Pastor, not priest and yes - I can date.

DEAN. How's that working out?

GRACE. Sort of dating a white guy that is into Buddhism. He keeps trying to get me to come to his meditation center.

DEAN. Do you drag him to church with you?

GRACE. No. But we both love The Bachelorette, so that's something.

DEAN. That show is such trash, but my sister and mom love it too.

GRACE. Yeah.

DEAN. New relationship?

GRACE. Yeah - I like him, but don't want to push too hard on the religion. Working on the cat thing too. He's more of a dog guy.

DEAN. So you're just sexting him all the time?

GRACE. *(Laughs.)* No! I don't really want to talk about my sex life with a teenager on my first day on the job.

DEAN. Your secret is safe with me. I'm going to be dead soon anyways.

GRACE. Shit, yeah - god I suck at this.

DEAN. No - you don't suck at comforting me. You're just talking to me. It's fine. Well - fine and not fine.

GRACE. Do you know the band - N-E-R-D?

DEAN. Hmm - I think so - what are their songs again?

GRACE. Lapdance, Rock Star, Party People.

DEAN. Damn - you like it raunchy.

GRACE. That's beside the point. But the acronym of the band is No-one Ever Really Dies.

DEAN. So I'll be getting lap dances as a rock star in heaven and hanging out with party people.

GRACE. Maybe?

DEAN. Not a bad way to spend the afterlife.

GRACE. Gotta be honest - life is fucked and weird and we're all trying to find meaning.

DEAN. Ha ha ha - I thought you were trying not to curse.

GRACE. Trying, but failing.

DEAN. Yeah - I feel you. *(Grace walks over to Dean and sits next to him. She grabs his hand.)*

GRACE. Thank you for being my first.

DEAN. What the hell? You're not going to pop my cherry. You're not really my type. *(Grace laughs and pushes her hand away from Dean's hand.)*

GRACE. No - I meant my first parishioner or first hospital patient.

DEAN. Oh gotcha.

GRACE. I'm going to mess up a lot, but I think I can handle this.

DEAN. Yeah - I'm the one dying and sometimes I feel like I can handle it better than my family.

GRACE. I'm not looking forward to all the folks I'm going to see crying.

DEAN. I'd hate that.

GRACE. Part of the job.

DEAN. Why do you want to work for a church?

GRACE. I dunno. I just have a sense of purpose. God feels like a warm hug when you're down or happy or just anxious. Like a big brother looking down on me.

DEAN. Sounds like a creeper spying on you. Don't you remember 1984?

GRACE. Mister literary!

DEAN. I had to read the book in English class last year. I was forced to be literary.

GRACE. Gotcha - I've read that book too. *(Dean hears a buzzing on his phone. He picks it up and then puts it back in his pocket.)*

DEAN. Shit - I've gotta go. My parents are asking about me.

GRACE. Don't they know where you are?

DEAN. After we talk to the doctors, I usually say I need to take a walk around to get fresh air or I need to go to the bathroom - but I've been coming here.

GRACE. I ruined your hiding spot.

DEAN. Nah - it's all good.

GRACE. I helped - sorta?

DEAN. Maybe. I don't know if I believe in God or not - but it's nice to listen to someone else's life that isn't tragic like mine for a little bit.

GRACE. I'm not a crazy cat lady.

DEAN. No worries - seriously - we have a fat ass tabby named Gabriel at home.

GRACE. Sounds cute.

DEAN. Blessed are those who mourn, for they will be comforted. *(Pause.)* I like that. I'll remember that passage from your book of answers.

GRACE. It's a good book.

DEAN. I've gotta go - but good luck on your new gig. I think you'll need it. *(He smiles and walks to the back of the church and exits. Grace flips back to the first passage in the bible she quoted.)*

GRACE. Blessed are those who mourn, for they will be comforted.

END OF PLAY

SÉANCE

By Dylan Horowitz

A gay couple, James and Garth, prepare a séance in order to summon James' deceased father. He has news to share but is a little anxious of how well his father will take it. (Comedy, 2M)

CHARACTERS

JAMES
Male, 20's; Calm, athletic, Garth's boyfriend.

GARTH
Male, 20's; Spiritual, loving, James' boyfriend.

SETTING

The home of Garth & James. They are preparing a séance.

***

At rise, Garth & James are preparing for a séance in their home. There is a table that Garth is preparing just so, with a candle in the center. James is anxiously pacing around the room.

James checks the time on his phone.

JAMES. It's nearly midnight, you know.

GARTH. *(Calmly, graceful.)* I am aware.

JAMES. We could still call it quits, head over to Sarah's party.

GARTH. We will! After this. *(Goes back to preparing.)*

JAMES. After this. Right. *(Continues pacing.)* It's just that ... well I mean look at me, I look ... Mm ... and you look ... mmMMm ... and we don't want to get there so late that everyone's too drunk to notice, you know? That's all it is. Yeah. That's it.

50

GARTH. You are way too wired. Have you smoked?

JAMES. No.

GARTH. *(Handing James his weed pen.)* Take a hit, it'll help you feel better.

JAMES. *(Wanting to.)* I can't.

GARTH. What do you mean you can't?

JAMES. I mean ... *(Whispering, as if hiding from someone who isn't there.)* he'll know.

GARTH. How's he gonna know?

JAMES. He just ... will.

GARTH. James. Baby. Sweetie. Sweetheart.

JAMES. I'm right here.

GARTH. Honey. Who's the expert, you or me?

JAMES. That would be you.

GARTH. Right! And I'm telling you, he's not gonna know.

JAMES. And I'm telling you, as the resident expert on ... him ... he's going to know. *(Garth makes a face. Pause.)* Okay fine, give me the pen. *(Garth smirks, relinquishing his pen into James' possession. James sits across from Garth at the table and takes a hit, slowly exhaling.)*

GARTH. Better, right?

JAMES. Shut up.

GARTH. Make me.

JAMES. One thing at a time, please.

GARTH. Bore.

JAMES. Whore.

GARTH. I love it when you talk dirty to me.

JAMES. Garth!

GARTH. Alright! Don't get your panties in a twist, we're ready.

JAMES. Okay. So what do I need to do?

GARTH. *(Guiding James.)* First we light the candle ... *(He does.)* there! Now take my hands. Perfect. Aww, isn't this romantic? Holding hands by the candlelight on all hallows eve!

JAMES. Ah yes, holding hands and summoning the dead. So romantic.

GARTH. I know! Now remember, once he's here you'll have five minutes at the most, so make it count. Got it?

JAMES. Got it.

GARTH. Good. Now, just repeat after me, okay?

JAMES. Okay.

GARTH. Okay. *(Clearing his throat.)* Salaca doo.

JAMES. Salaca doo.

GARTH. La menthicka boo.

JAMES. La menthicka boo.

GARTH. La bibbidi-bobbidi-boo.

JAMES. La ... what?

GARTH. Put 'em together and what have you got?

JAMES. *(Unamused.)* ... bibbidi-bobbidi boo.

GARTH. *(Laughing hysterically.)* You're so adorable!

JAMES. Look, if you're not going to take this seriously -

GARTH. Okay, okay! For real this time. "Spirits near and dear to me, let borrowed voice come set you free."

JAMES. Spirits near and dear to me, let borrowed voice come set you free.

GARTH. Keep repeating it. *(James repeats the line.)* Focus on the words, what they mean. Think about your intention, who you're trying to summon, your emotions surrounding him, your feelings. *(The light on the table flickers.)* Great! Now focus those feelings into a little ball of energy, right in front of you. Put it all there, all those feelings, those sentiments and just - push! *(There's a great lightning-like flash as Garth shakes and seizes. It's as if he's having a seizure. James let's go of Garth's hands.)*

JAMES. Did it work?

GARTH (POSSESSED). *(Taking a deep breath.)* JAMES GUTHRIE MASTERSON!

JAMES. Hi, dad.

GARTH (POSSESSED). I ACCEPT YOUR SUMMONS TO THIS MORTAL PLANE FOR I HAVE UNFINISHED BUSINESS OF WHICH YOU MUST - have you been smoking weed?

JAMES. ...no?

GARTH (POSSESSED). James Guthrie Masterson, are you lying to me?

JAMES. ...maybe. *(Garth (Possessed) extends his hand, miming for James to give him the pen. James, rolling his eyes, does so. Garth (Possessed) is confused for a moment by the pen not being a blunt before shrugging it off and putting it in his (as in Garth's) pocket.)* Dad, there's something I need to tell -

GARTH (POSSESSED). SILENCE, SON OF MINE!

JAMES. Orrr not.

GARTH (POSSESSED). JAMES GUTHRIE MASTERSON.

JAMES. You can just say James, dad.

GARTH (POSSESSED). JAMES GUTHRIE MASTERSON, I HAVE LEFT UNFINISHED BUSINESS UPON THIS MORTAL COIL. AS MY SOLE HEIR, YOU SHALL FINISH IT FOR ME.

JAMES. Yeah, that's all well and good, Dad, but there's kind of something important I need to tell -

GARTH (POSSESSED). FIRST!

JAMES. Why do I even ...

GARTH (POSSESSED). IN THE SECOND DRAWER OF MY STUDY RESTS MY PERSONAL COMPUTER.

JAMES. Yeah, Dad, I know about the furry porn.

GARTH (POSSESSED). YOU ARE TO GO FORTH AND DELETE MY BROWSER - you what?

JAMES. Yeah, I know about the furry porn. Everybody knows about the furry porn.

GARTH (POSSESSED). How?!

JAMES. Because you would watch it with the volume all the way up without headphones!

GARTH (POSSESSED). ...oh. Nevermind, then.

JAMES. Great, now can I please say what I called you here to talk -

GARTH (POSSESSED). SECOND!

JAMES. Dad, I'm gay!

GARTH (POSSESSED). I NEED YOU TO FIND JERRY SANDLER AND - I'm sorry, you're what?

JAMES. Gay, Dad, I'm gay.

GARTH (POSSESSED). You're - you're gay?

JAMES. Yes.

GARTH (POSSESSED). Are you sure?

JAMES. Pretty positive, Dad.

GARTH (POSSESSED). Well. Talk about a shock to the system!

JAMES. You're a ghost talking to your son from beyond the dead and me being gay is the biggest shock of the night for you?

GARTH (POSSESSED). Listen, supernatural phenomena that laugh at god and the laws of reality are one thing but this, well ... I mean ... gay??

JAMES. Look, dad, I know you might be feeling a bit disappointed right now but -

GARTH (POSSESSED). Disappointed? I'm just surprised! You were such a straight arrow growing up! Always went to all the football games, didn't miss a single one!

JAMES. Yep, not a single one.

GARTH (POSSESSED). And there was that girl you dated, the really pretty one, what's-her-face.

JAMES. What's-her-face?

GARTH (POSSESSED). What's-her-face! You know, you went to prom together, you'd go on dates - she used to drive around in that old Subaru.

JAMES. Ellen?

GARTH (POSSESSED). *(Claps hands.)* Ellen! That's it, Ellen. You loved Ellen.

JAMES. That I did, Dad. Ellen and Ellen's very big Subaru.

GARTH (POSSESSED). Right, so you see why this is such a shock for me.

JAMES. There is something else I need to tell you, Dad.

GARTH (POSSESSED). I mean where do you even get it from? It makes no sense!

JAMES. Dad -

GARTH (POSSESSED). Look at - no, son, this is important - look at me! *(Pointing at Garth.)* There is not a single gay bone in my body. *(Looks down. Beat.)* Who's body am I in?

JAMES. That would be my boyfriend's.

GARTH (POSSESSED). Y-y-y-y-your boyfriend's?

JAMES. Yes. Dad, meet ... Garth.

GARTH (POSSESSED). *(Nauseous.)* Oh ... uh ... He's your ... I think I'm gonna be sick.

JAMES. Dad!

GARTH (POSSESSED). Oh, I'm gonna hurl. Mhm. Yep. Definitely gonna hurl.

JAMES. Could you at least try and be nice about it? He's my boyfriend and I love him.

GARTH (POSSESSED). Yes, exactly! He's your

boyfriend! And I'm your father! *(Silence. James is confused.)* In your boyfriend's body! *(Further silence. James isn't taking the hint.)* YOU'VE. HAD. SEX. WITH. THIS. BODY.

JAMES. *(Beat.)* I see your point.

GARTH (POSSESSED). You know what? I-I think I'm gonna go.

JAMES. Dad -

GARTH (POSSESSED). No, no it's okay, you don't have to do that unfinished business stuff. This is just, um ... *(Looking down again.)* eghh.

JAMES. Look dad, before you go -

GARTH (POSSESSED). Listen, son, I get you've got more to say to your old man but uh ... m yep. Lunch is comin' up, gotta go.

JAMES. It's really important you hear this.

GARTH (POSSESSED). Tell you what, summon your mother and she can *(Looking down a third time.)* ... well, maybe don't tell her that bit but uh -

JAMES. WE'RE ENGAGED! *(Beat. It's as if everything has frozen. The words ring in James' father's head, making him forget everything else including his nausea).*

GARTH (POSSESSED). *(Excited.)* My baby boy's getting married? *(James nods his head, happily. Before his father can say anything, the room trembles and there are lightning flashes as Garth's body spasms once again. Eventually everything calms down. Garth, returned, raises his head to meet James' gaze.)*

GARTH. So ... how did it go?

JAMES. *(Beat.)* I think he took it well.

END OF PLAY

SURVIVORS

By John David Brown

How honest are we allowed to be after someone has died—honest about the deceased, and honest about ourselves? After the passing of his wife, Russ is confronted by his mother-in-law about his unruly actions at the funeral service. (Dark Comedy, 1M, 1W)

CHARACTERS

TANYA
Female, 40's-70's; Russ's mother-in-law. Reserved and stoic.

RUSS
Male, 20s-30s; Tanya's son-in-law. In the middle of a breakdown.

SETTING

A private area at a funeral service.

***

At rise, Tanya pulls Russ onstage.

TANYA. What did you say to Ms. Johnson?

RUSS. *(Sarcastically.)* Calm down, Tanya. You don't want them to hear you in the sanctuary.

TANYA. Do not start with me, Russ. Not today.

RUSS. You're not having a great time at your daughter's funeral? Because so far, my wife's funeral has been an absolute hoot.

TANYA. That poor lady looked like she was about to have a heart attack. And she's ninety-one, so that's a very real possibility.

RUSS. Oh please. She's lived through five wars and a black president. I don't think one conversation with me is gonna

57

do her in. Honestly, she's the one who said something offensive to me.

TANYA. *(She does not believe him.)* Really. What did she say?

RUSS. So I'm standing here beside a coffin which holds, you know, Sarah's dead body, and she totters up to me and says, "Are you doing okay?"

TANYA. *(Confused pause.)* She just asked you how you were doing?

RUSS. No, she asked me if I was doing "okay."

TANYA. I must be missing something here. Did she spit on you after she said it?

RUSS. Of course I'm not doing okay! I'm at the funeral of my wife, my young, dead wife. I've been a widower for three days. I am the newly single father to a two-year-old daughter. But yeah, I'm feeling just peachy.

TANYA. Did you, by chance, communicate these feelings to Ms. Johnson?

RUSS. All I said was, "No, I'm not doing okay."

TANYA. That's all you said?

RUSS. Yes.

TANYA. So why did she have to lay down in the pew when she got done talking to you?

RUSS. Well … then she said for me to let her know if I needed anything. So I told her.

TANYA. You told her what?

RUSS. I told her what I needed.

TANYA. Which was?

RUSS. About $45,000 a year, because that was Sarah's salary.

TANYA. Oh no.

RUSS. And then I said I could really use a cigarette.

TANYA. Russ, I swear.

RUSS. And then I said I needed her to teach me whatever witchcraft she's been using to stay alive for the last thousand years because maybe if we tweaked the spell it could bring my wife back from the dead.

TANYA. *(She takes a long moment before she responds.)* Russ, you and I have not always seen eye to eye. If I'm being honest, I can't say that I was particularly thrilled when you and Sarah got married.

RUSS. Yeah, I don't like you either. It's fine.

TANYA. Great. That being said, this is a very difficult day for a lot of people. So I'm going to ask that, for once in your life, you don't make everything all about you.

RUSS. Make everything about me? Today, everything is absolutely about me. My wife is dead. Suddenly. With no warning. My favorite person who has ever lived was taken from me. And you want me to be polite? You want me to shake hands and hug necks and pretend that I'm doing ... okay?

TANYA. *(Somehow still not getting hysterical.)* What about me? Sarah was my daughter, my perfect, precious, beautiful daughter. She was my favorite person first. I am not saying that you are not hurting, because I know you are. But ... you can't understand the devastation of losing a child. A spouse is one thing, but a child...they're not supposed to go first. They are a part of yourself that you release out into the world so they can keep going after you're gone. And when they die before you do ... you die too. So don't think for one second that you're the only one who's hurting here.

RUSS. Hey, I don't think that. She was your daughter. I know that.

TANYA. And yet, here I am, not emotionally terrorizing old people.

RUSS. But that's the thing! You should be! If you're so devastated, then act devastated! Get mad! Flip a table! Set something on fire! This is what's making me absolutely insane. Why am I the only one who's spiraling out of control?

TANYA. Russ, you're always out of control.

RUSS. Honestly, that's fair. I'm not the world's most stable person on a good day. And you've got resting brave face. I get that. But come on. You've got a dead daughter now. At the very least, you could cry. I haven't seen you cry once in the past three days. No one has. We're all talking about it. It's freaking us out.

TANYA. Who is "we?"

RUSS. Everyone. Your kids, the preacher, every person in this church today. The second you're out of earshot, people are like, "Tanya's running around like she's planning a Women's Club luncheon."

TANYA. Are they really saying that?

RUSS. Yes! You haven't stopped running around since the second Sarah died. You called the florist from the hospital parking lot.

TANYA. We were going to need flowers for the service.

RUSS. You don't buy flowers for your own daughter's funeral! Other people do that for you!

TANYA. Sarah liked yellow roses.

RUSS. That's like the most common funeral flower! Everyone would've sent yellow roses!

TANYA. Well I am sorry that I wanted to make sure Sarah got the funeral she deserved.

RUSS. *(Pause.)* But this isn't about Sarah, is it? It can't be. There's no her for this to be about anymore.

TANYA. Don't say that.

RUSS. It's true. She's not still with us. We're not gonna feel her in the breeze. She's gone on to bigger and better things. So no, this isn't about her. This is about the people who are left behind. We have to do what we can to survive. I loved Sarah more than anything. I would've done anything for her. I did do anything for her when she was alive. I turned down job offers and stayed in this town and lived next to you. You! And I was happy to do it. Because she was everything to me. But she's dead. The goal of my life isn't to honor her memory or make her happy anymore. I've got to survive in a world without her now. And so do you. This isn't about Sarah because it's about me and you.

TANYA. I don't want this to be about me. I don't want to think about anything that's happening to me right now. If I seem like I'm running around crazy, it's because I can't sit in the middle of all of this. If I don't keep moving, it's going to catch me. I can't let that happen. Not yet. Because if I sit down right now, I'm scared I'll never get back up again.

RUSS. *(Pause.)* Okay. That's fair. *(Pause.)* But I don't know how not to sit in the middle of it. I don't have anywhere to run. It's everywhere. My future with her. All the plans we had. Our daughter. We have a daughter. Well, I have a daughter. And she doesn't have a mother. And I don't have a wife. And now all these people are coming up to me and asking if I'm okay. What a stupid question. What an absolutely moronic thing to say. It would be one thing if they actually wanted to know, if they were giving me permission to be honest. But they're not. My wife just died, and they want me to be like, "You know, it's gonna be tough, but we'll make it through." No. I'm not doing it. I'm not going to make today about their comfort. I'm sorry I almost killed Ms. Johnson. She was probably not the right vessel for my wrath. But I don't know how to play nice right now. I don't have any nice left in me. And I get what you're saying, but isn't there a tiny part of you that doesn't want to play hostess right now? Don't you feel just an inkling of anger every time someone asks if you're doing okay?

TANYA. No. *(Pause.)* Maybe. I don't know. *(Pause.)* It is a stupid question.

RUSS. Thank you.

TANYA. But you can't burn down your whole life. A lot of people are gonna say a lot of stupid things to you, especially over the next few months. You can't destroy them all.

RUSS. I don't know. Sounds kinda fun.

TANYA. Russ.

RUSS. I get it, okay? And I know things will get better. I hope so, anyway. But today. I don't know how not to destroy people today.

TANYA. *(Long pause.)* Do you have a pen?

RUSS. Um, I actually do. *(He pulls a pen out of his pocket as she fishes a scrap of paper out of her purse. He hands her the pen, and she writes as she talks.)*

TANYA. If you're amenable to it, I have a solution.

RUSS. *(Unsure.)* Okay.

TANYA. I'm writing down the names of three people. I won't survive today if you psychologically abuse everyone who tries to talk to you. My nerves can't handle it. That's just how it is. But these three people are fair game. They can be the sin eaters for all the torment you need to inflict. So?

RUSS. Who are they? *(She hands him the list.)* Jared Buskins. Samantha Smith. Pastor Rick. *(He looks at her in delighted surprise.)* Pastor Rick?

TANYA. One time when Sarah was a teenager, he called her out in front of the entire church because he said her skirt was too short. It was, but I've hated him ever since.

RUSS. After I'm done with him, he's gonna have to leave the ministry. Who are the other two?

TANYA. Samantha is my old boss. Hateful woman. And

Jared is actually my second cousin. He's very racist. I mean very, very racist.

RUSS. And they're all here?

TANYA. Yep.

RUSS. *(Pause.)* I think I can make this work.

TANYA. Like you said, we have to figure out how to survive. So let's survive today. *(They start to head back into the sanctuary.)*

RUSS. Sarah would've liked this.

TANYA. Liked what?

RUSS. Us. *(Tanya freezes.)*

TANYA. Oh no.

RUSS. What's wrong? *(Tanya starts to cry.)*

TANYA. Dang it dang it dang it dang it. Not yet.

RUSS. Hey. It's okay.

TANYA. No! If I get started …

RUSS. Look at me. Tanya, look at me. We are going to go out there, and I am going to murder these three people, and you are going to put your brave face back on and make small talk and play nice with all of these idiots who don't know what we're going through. Okay?

TANYA. *(Pulling herself together.)* Okay.

RUSS. In a couple of hours, you'll be home, and you can lock your bedroom door and let all of this out. But for right now, for the next hour, we are going to survive.

TANYA. Okay. Okay. I'm okay.

RUSS. No you're not. But let's go anyway. *(They exit together.)*

END OF PLAY

THE ELUSIVE PURSUIT OF MAXIMIM BLISS

By Ken Pruess

A researcher and her wealthy benefactor, both missing something in their lives, explore multiple timelines to find the feasibility of 100% happiness. (Sci-fi, 1M, 1W)

CHARACTERS

MAX
Male. A rich man seeking the secret to achieving 100% happiness.

ELLE
Female. A caring scientist offering a glimpse at alternate timelines and ultimate bliss.

SETTING

A scientific lab in a not-too-distant future

NOTES

The set consists of a small table or tray to house a laptop and a few small items, a chair, and an unseen fourth wall upon which actors view projections. Lighting effects to help sell the idea the projections may be added but are not essential.

***

At rise, Max enters the room, greeted by a slightly nervous Elle.

ELLE. Mr. Chance.

MAX. Please, call me Max.

ELLE. *(Tries it out.)* Max. I'm Elle. *(Notices her sweaty hand; wipes it off; embarrassed.)* And I'm nervous.

MAX. No need to be. *(A beat followed by a playful smile.)* I've already given you my money.

ELLE. Yes. You have. Your grant meant so much. *(A bit of doubt.)* I just hope I don't disappoint you.

MAX. *(A reassuring smile with a hint of tenderness.)* It already feels like money well spent. *(Awkward beat as he wonders if he's been too flirty. Elle blushes wondering if she misinterpreted his words.)*

ELLE. Come in then. I'll show you what I've got. *(Her face shows a slight regret with her choice of words.)*

MAX. *(Looks around the room.)* So, this is where the magic happens?

ELLE. I hope so. Guess we'll find out for sure. Any electronic devices on you?

MAX. My phone and my Bliss-Band. *(He rolls up his sleeve to reveal a watch-like device. He peeks at the face.)* 86%. Up a tick since I got here. Something's cheered me up a bit.

ELLE. Probably the smell of chocolate chip cookies.

MAX. *(Smiles.)* My favorite. Have any left?

ELLE. Never had any. It's just a fragrance spray to make the lab feel homey.

MAX. *(Looks at watch.)* And I am back down to 85. *(Sighs.)* Pretty consistent for me these days.

ELLE. Impressive number. *(Slides sleeve to reveal a Bliss-Band.)* My happiness hovers in the high 70s.

MAX. I should've brought you real chocolate chips.

ELLE. *(Laughs.)* That would've helped. *(A beat.)* The band will be distracting though. You mind taking it off?

MAX. Taking it off is easy. Leaving it off is the issue. *(He removes it and hands it to her.)* Damn things are an addiction. Always checking the percentage …

ELLE. *(Sets Bliss-Band on table. Sneaks peek at hers.)* Seeing how it corresponds with your current activity ...

MAX. … waiting for that elusive 100% chime.

ELLE. It's a bit consuming, isn't it?

MAX. I think we were all happier before we had a device to tell us how happy we were.

ELLE. I think you're right. I heard one once, though. The 100% chime. Several years back now. A couple with a dog across the park near my home. It inspired my research. It was lovely.

MAX. Was it real, though? They were probably actors strategically planted to trick people into believing it's possible. 100% happy. I can't see it happening.

ELLE. Well, not from here. Let's get started and see if we can change that.

MAX. That's the kind of can-do attitude I admire.

ELLE. And funded generously.

MAX. You tried this all out on yourself first, right?

ELLE. I haven't, actually. Too nervous, I guess. It's difficult …

MAX. … to be both subject and observer.

ELLE. And to take it all in. *(She wants to say more but opts against it.)* So … *(Gestures to a chair, center.)* … you'll sit here, so you can see the images on the wall. *(Points to a downstage wall a few feet away.)*

MAX. And … take it all in.

ELLE. Right. *(Moves to computer. Hits keys.)* I won't bore you with the science I included in my proposal.

MAX. And I won't lie to you by pretending I understood it.

ELLE. *(Pauses data entry.)* You read it, didn't you?

MAX. Enough to see we were seeking the same thing. *(Looks around.)* You were really a schoolteacher before you built all this?

ELLE. *(Nods.)* High school science. I just felt there was

something missing.

MAX. A paycheck? Respect? A lunchbreak?

ELLE. *(Smiles.)* All that. But more. There was … *(Searches for the right word.)*

MAX. An emptiness. I sensed it in your writing. That's why I'm here. Kindred spirit.

ELLE. Benefactor.

MAX. Lab rat.

ELLE. *(Corrects him.)* Guinea pig.

MAX. I like that better. Guinea pigs are cuter.

ELLE. I think so. *(There is a beat as they look at each other. She moves on.)* Left paw please. *(She slides a device on his left ring finger: An untethered thimble that fits snugly.)*

MAX. *(Raises a hand to examine it.)* Small device for such a substantial endeavor.

ELLE. It packs a punch. Trust me. *(Hits keys. Points downstage.)* In about ten seconds, the wall will fill with images.

MAX. *(There is a subtle light change.)* That's me. *(His head moves left to right as he scans across the top row of the wall.)* Lots of me. *(His head moves down slightly as he scans more, taking in several stacked rows of images.)* I didn't pose for these. Is this photoshop?

ELLE. Not exactly.

MAX. I don't understand.

ELLE. Then just … feel. *(She touches his shoulder. He looks at her. She lifts her hand, steps forward, and points.)* These are the first hundred.

MAX. First hundred?

ELLE There are millions here. *(She swipes her hand in the air, manipulating the wall as one would a smart phone. She swipes several times. Their eyes (and perhaps lights) suggest several screens passing by.)*

MAX. What are they?

ELLE. Variations of you. In alternate timelines. Concurrent realities. A new one is generated every time you make a choice.

MAX. *(Stands and moves up to her side.)* You're kidding.

ELLE. *(Shakes head.)* There's a you somewhere now who decided to remain seated in that chair.

MAX. *(Looks from chair to the screen, taking it all in.)* I look pretty similar in all of these.

ELLE. Same age. Right down to the minute. If you look closely though, you'll see little differences. *(Searches then points.)* Scar above the eye. *(Searches then points.)* Pierced ear. *(Searches then points.)* Questionable mustache.

MAX. Combine those three, I'd be quite the pirate. *(A beat.)* So, my life is different in each of these timelines?

ELLE. Slightly in some. Vastly in others. I'll show you an example. Choose a variant.

MAX. *(Points.)* Gotta go with the Mustache Max.

ELLE. *(She reaches out as if selecting the image. She slides it center of the wall then flicks her fingers open as if enlarging it. She leans and reads from the image.)* 3-13-76-1420.

MAX. What's that?

ELLE *(Moves to the keyboard.)* The M.O.D. Moment of Divergence. Its time stamped in the corner. *(Typing in as she speaks.)* March 13, 1976, 2:20 pm. You and Mustache Max lived the exact same life until it diverged at this moment. *(She hits a key. They both react to an image that appears center.)*

MAX. *(Taken aback.)* Is this a photo?

ELLE. A rendering. Based on your memory.

MAX. I'd forgotten all about this.

ELLE. Not subconsciously.

MAX. My mother looks so young.

ELLE. This is the view as seen through your eyes. *(Consults her screen.)* She's asking you to …

MAX. … choose between piano lessons and baseball.

ELLE. You remember then?

MAX. I do now. There wasn't enough time for both. *(A realization.)* I suppose there wasn't enough money, either. I chose piano.

ELLE. *(Points to screen.)* Mustache Max chose baseball.

MAX. And, he had a different life?

ELLE. A million different lives. *(Hits keys. Max's eyes widen. His head moves as before, watching the wall populate with a hundred new images. Elle peeks at wall and points as she references each image.)* Number 1 quit after tryouts. Number 2 lasted four practices. Number 3 broke his nose opening day.

MAX. *(Grimaces slightly.)* Wild pitch or line drive?

ELLE. *(Consults.)* Tripped on the pitcher's mound walking to the dugout from right field.

MAX. *(Laughs.)* I'm guessing none of them made it to the major leagues.

ELLE. Infinite timelines generally allow for infinite realities. But, in this particular case, no.

MAX. Choosing piano didn't make me a rock star either.

ELLE. *(Points to Max.)* Not the version of you that's standing here. But if we explore the variants who diverged sometime after you chose piano, *(Hits keys. Looks at wall.)* there are clearly some variants here with rock-n-roll hair. *(Points.)* Is that a mullet?

MAX. Wait. Stop. I don't want to see.

ELLE. It's not that bad of a haircut.

MAX. No. I don't want to see that I could have been a rock star. I have enough regrets in my own life. I don't need to add more from alternate timelines. *(Crosses to the desk and holds up his Bliss-Band. He waits a second for it to calibrate.)* 84%. We're supposed to be raising my bliss not lowering it. *(Sets it down. Calms himself.)* Are we wasting our time? Is 100% even feasible?

ELLE. I'm confident it is.

MAX. Why? Because you saw a phantom couple across the park by your house? *(Before she can answer.)* Maybe you should show me the variants whose lives went horribly wrong, so I'll feel happier by comparison. Is there a Heart Attack Max? A Mountain Man Max who was mauled by a bear? *(Points to screen.)* Look at Mullet Max. There's got to be a timeline where he OD'd after getting fired from his Billy Ray Cyrus cover band.

ELLE. I could show you those kind of things, if you'd like. Or, as originally planned, I could show you these. *(Hits keys. Points to wall.)* The variants who achieved 100% happiness.

MAX. What? *(He looks at the wall.)* They … *(A serious beat.)* there's only … seven.

ELLE. It's not an easy task.

MAX. Why were these able to do it when millions of Maxes couldn't. *(A beat.)* When I couldn't.

ELLE. Every soul finds happiness in its own way. Relationships. Wealth. Success. Fame. Religion. Charity. Travel. Art. No path is superior or inferior. Just different. These were the lucky ones who found what they needed.

MAX. And … you can show me what made each of them happy?

ELLE. I can try … if you're sure you want to see.

MAX. That's why I'm here, right? Why I paid for all these resources. To find what's missing in my life.

ELLE. I know that 100% happiness sounds perfect ...

MAX. It is perfect.

ELLE. But what if it's fleeting? Who knows how long it'll last? You're 85% happy. Consistently. You said so yourself.

MAX. But I feel I could be happier. I want to be happier. I'd regret not going for it.

ELLE. What if you reach 100% and then it fades. Wouldn't that be a bigger regret? You risk spending the rest of your life obsessed, trying to reach that same high again.

MAX. I've been obsessed ever since I got that Bliss-Band. I've done everything I can in hopes of hearing that chime. That emptiness. The kind I sensed in you. Wouldn't you like to escape it? Even if it's temporary?

ELLE. I suppose. *(Quickly.)* I don't know. This is why I'm the observer and not the subject.

MAX. *(Calmly, to show her that he's good with his decision.)* Let's observe one and see what happens. *(Points.)* How about Max in the Middle?

ELLE. *(Looks up, trying to relax into the moment.)* That's a nice tan. Let's hope it's real.

MAX. *(Shoots her a smile.)* Says the woman who sprays cookies from a can.

ELLE. *(Smiles back. Looks at computer.)* Let's see. You diverged at a traffic light in 2001. You stopped. He kept going.

MAX. *(Almost to himself.)* I've probably played things too safe. *(To Elle.)* What happened next?

ELLE. Millions of choices. Significant and insignificant. Ultimately leading him to the moment of 100% happiness. *(Hits key. Looks up.)*

MAX. *(Awed by the view.)* That's ... a ... beautiful ... sunset.

ELLE. Spectacular. *(Moves in closer to him.)* Where are you, though?

MAX. I can't tell. *(Looks to her.)* Is there another view?

ELLE. I can only render the memory through his eyes.

MAX. Well, I'm obviously sitting with someone. Unless I've grown an extra left foot and painted my toenails.

ELLE. I'd be impressed if you did. That's my shade of ... *(Suddenly.)* Wait a second. That's my foot.

MAX. What?

ELLE. That's my foot! I've seen it many times. The polish. The little toe that hides behind its neighbor. I think you're sitting with me. *(Max glances at Elle's shoes then back to the screen. She moves to the computer.)* I'm bringing up another one. *(Hits keys. Looks up.)* Oh my.

MAX. *(Looks at her.)* What? *(Looks at wall.)* That's my television. I have no idea what I'm watching though.

ELLE. It's Amelie. My favorite movie. And that's the same foot on the coffee table.

MAX. Bring up the rest. All together.

ELLE. *(Hitting keys.)* Already working on it. *(More images appear. She moves to his side. Their eyes widen, looking across the wall.)* It's me.

MAX. It's you.

ELLE. It's us. *(There's a silent beat as they review the images. A smile slowly blooms on Max's face.)*

MAX. Not to overstep my role in this experiment, but you're clearly the catalyst in six of these. I don't know about the dog image. Maybe he just made me super happy. I've kind of always loved Boston Terriers.

ELLE. Me, too. That's Serendipity.

MAX. *(Looks at her sweetly.)* It certainly is.

ELLE. *(Laughs.)* No. I named her Serendipity. I've had her

for years. We're clearly walking her in the park near my home. *(They pause a moment, thinking about her words.)*

MAX. Think you should look at your 100-Percents?

ELLE. I think I will. I've got a good idea what I'll see, though. *(Sneaks a peek at her Bliss-Band.)* I'm really enjoying these at the moment. *(They move closer together as they look at the wall.)*

MAX. So, what do we make of these results?

ELLE. Well, evidence suggests that your soul finds optimum bliss …

MAX. … when it realizes it's found the person it's destined to be with.

ELLE. Seems like a solid hypothesis.

MAX. One worthy of a final test. *(He crosses to the table and picks up his Bliss-Band. He places it on his wrist and returns to Elle. He takes both of her hands into his and looks into her eyes. There is a silent, tender moment of anticipation followed by a soft, lovely chime. Max lifts his hand as the couple listens to his band. There is a hint of a dance as the chime plays and fades.)*

ELLE. There's no proof this will last forever, you know.

MAX. There's no proof it won't.

ELLE. You're willing to take the risk?

MAX. One hundred percent. *(There is a new chime. This one emanating from Elle's Bliss-Band. She holds up her left hand. They smile and listen together. Elle reaches out her other hand and hits a few keys. Max slips the thimble off his hand onto her finger, almost like a ring. They move closer together, her head on his shoulders, to watch her 100-Percents appear. Their eyes widen, their smiles do as well, as the lights fade to black.)*

END OF PLAY

WHAT THE HELL IS GOING ON?

By Julian Diaz

After living a peaceful life of no real consequence, a regular person just like you or I finds themselves in the afterlife, but it utterly defies expectation. There are no angels, no pearly gates, and no God. At least, the person that currently holds the title doesn't really measure up. As our protagonist tries to unravel the tangled headphones that are the answer to humanity's greatest question, it becomes painfully clear that not even God knows what the hell is going on. (Comedy, 2 any gender)

CHARACTERS

DEAD PERSON
Recently deceased. Overwhelmed by the revelation that the afterlife is so chaotic and stressful. Literally made of questions. No fixed gender or ethnicity.

GOD (or something like it)
A bafflingly powerful being doing their best. Overworked, overstressed, and desperately in need of a reprieve. No fixed gender or ethnicity.

SETTING

The ostensible afterlife. It is a featureless void inhabited by one individual responsible for looking out its only window into the universe and controlling almost everything by hand.

NOTES

The fact that both characters are normal, unspecial, people wearing identical costumes is intentional and integral to the central theme. To keep things from getting confusing or, more importantly, boring for the audience, try to cast people from two (at minimum) unique backgrounds and with easily discernible characteristics.

***

At rise, a lone person is laying on the stage dressed all in white. They appear to be sleeping peacefully. Angelic harps and singing birds are heard.

Dead Person slowly wakes up from a peaceful sleep, yawning and stretching to greet the afterlife.

DEAD. Woah ... I ... I died! That was it, I felt it! It was so ... peaceful. *(He looks around at the afterlife, finding it a featureless void that also happens to be blindingly white.)* Damn ... guess I was wrong about there being an afterlife. Welp. I guess it's time to pay for all that weird porn on my laptop. Go on Satan, do your worst. Just know I'm WAY into this. *(He assumes a position that is ready to receive some manner of existentially baffling, and probably a little gross, punishment. There is no reply nor blazing inferno. There is only silence.]* What, nothing? Really? *(There is still no answer.)* Cool, thanks universe. This was fully worth 40 years of taxes and anxiety. *(Mumbling.)* Fucking ripoff ... *(A loud crash from offstage.)* Jesus! What the hell was that?

GOD. *(Offstage.)* OH SHIT! NO! DAMMIT! FUCK FUCK FUCK!

DEAD. What the ... *(God comes stumbling in from off stage, dressed identically to Dead Person. They are in a panic, spewing expletives as they come crashing onto the stage. They do not seem to notice Dead Person.]*

GOD. *(Ad lib.)* FUCK! SHIT! NO NO NO NO!!! *(Stares out into the audience, where there is a window into the universe.)* GOD DAMMIT! I go to take a shit for ONE second and these motherfuckers have destroyed the freaking O-Zone layer again. Uuugh! Okay okay … this is fine … I'll just send down another Ghandi or Thunberg or something and hope they listen to this one. Maybe if I make this one from an English-speaking country they won't become a meme.

DEAD. Um … excuse me? Are you in charge here?

GOD. *(Shocked.)* What?!

DEAD. I just … I just got here and I don't know what I'm supposed to be doing.

GOD. Holy shit … It's finally happened … After all these eons … *(God reaches for Dead Person to touch their face and inspect them.)*

DEAD. W-what happened?

GOD. I've gone completely fucking insane. This is sooner than I thought it would be but then again I stopped keeping time about a billion years ago. *(Dead Person jerks away from God's hands.)*

DEAD. What? No, listen pal I'm not a hallucination. I'm dead. I think …

GOD. Dead? Wait … You're from earth? Like, down there?

DEAD. I guess so? I mean, yes, I'm from earth but why does that -

GOD. Oh man … oh man oh man oh man … This is unprecedented. No one's ever come here before …

DEAD. What do you mean? Isn't this the afterlife?

GOD. Yes … and no. You're not supposed to be here though … shit, how did I fuck that up? UGH! I don't have time to sort this out, I'm trying to get these morons to stop inventing new kinds of crypto currency. *(Shouting into the window.)* IT'S JUST VENMO FOR HUMAN TRAFFICKERS!

DEAD. Hey, sorry, I can see you're in the middle of some

kind of breakdown and I'd love to let you get back to it but I just wanna know which way heaven is.

GOD. What? Heaven? No, there's no heaven. But if there was it'd probably be full of plastic like my fucking oceans! Looking at you, The Philippines!! *(God goes back to the window, waving his hands and mumbling to himself.)*

DEAD. Plastic …? Wait hold on, what do you mean there's no heaven?

GOD. Not a thing, man. When you die it's just nothingness for eternity. Hate to break to ya. Had my hands so full with this earth shit I never got around to crafting an eternal paradise. But it's on my vision board I swear.

DEAD. That can't be right … how am I here then?

GOD. *(Tearing himself away from the window for a second.)* I literally have no idea! Okay?! I don't have any answers for you. We're both confused, the only difference is I'm keeping it moving while you're beating the hell out of a thoroughly dead horse. Can we please move on? There is no heaven, you're not supposed to be here, I'm God, shit is hitting the fan at a rate faster than my mind can comprehend so can I PLEASE get back to work?! *(There is a tense moment of silence.)*

DEAD. You're God?!

GOD. Oh for … Fine! *(God waves his hands at the window. The sound of a UFO flying by.)* There, I just gave them evidence of aliens, that should distract them for a few months. If you've got questions, let's just get it out of your system. Take a seat. *(Mystical magical sounds of a spell being invoked. Chairs slide in from off stage for the characters to sit in. God sits down while Dead Person is stunned for a moment.)* … well?

DEAD. I … I'm so sorry I forgot what I was gonna say.

GOD. That's it! *(God tries to go back to the window but Dead Person stops them.)*

DEAD. No wait! I remembered!

GOD. Go on.

DEAD. Okay so … you're God.

GOD. Yes. Well no. But in a broader sense yes.

DEAD. Okay, but this isn't heaven?

GOD. No this is just where I live and work. It's pretty nice. I've got my window, these chairs, and … *(He trails off trying to think of anything else.)*

DEAD. And how do -

GOD. And my pinball machine.

DEAD. … right. So, what, you control everything?

GOD. Basically, yeah.

DEAD. Everything?

GOD. Everything.

DEAD. Like … the weather and stuff?

GOD. That's a little reductionist but … yeah. Weather, the tides, ice cream machines at McDonalds. Shit like that.

DEAD. Wait so you're in control of everyone's actions and everything they do?

GOD. Oh no no not that.

DEAD. But you said you control everything.

GOD. Yeah everything but that.

DEAD. Why can't you do that?

GOD. Ugh … it was … I thought it would be easier to automate some of the processes on earth so I didn't have to have my hands in literally every pie but it kinda got out of hand. They started inventing fire and killing each other over the most inane shit, pretty quickly after it happened actually … worst decision I ever made and I have NO idea how to turn it off.

DEAD. Turn it off? What, free will?

GOD. Free will … that's way better than what I was calling it.

DEAD. What were you -

GOD. Stupid asshole syndrome.

DEAD. That's … alright that's fair. Alright, let me get this straight. Everything that happens on earth that isn't the fault of humans is you?

GOD. Yup.

DEAD. Earthquakes?

GOD. Yup, that's me.

DEAD. Famine?

GOD. All me.

DEAD. The Black Death?

GOD. Woah, haha, deep cut. But yeah that was me too.

DEAD. Covid-19?

GOD. No, that was the 5G towers actually. Yeah no the nutjobs were really batting a thousand that year. Wait till you hear about what they put in vaccines.

DEAD. Okay what about bone cancer in children?

GOD. *(Slightly embarrassed.)* Yeeeeeah.

DEAD. Why?

GOD. Why?

DEAD. Why?! Why do such awful things to children who have literally done nothing wrong in their short, innocent, lives?!

GOD. Well because it says to. In the manual.

DEAD. There's a fucking manual?

GOD. Yeah! You wanna see it?

DEAD. I … yes?

GOD. Here you go! *(He reaches into his pocket, making a show of rummaging around before pulling out his empty hand and giving Dead Peron the finger and making a fart noise at him.)*

DEAD. Oh real mature …

GOD. Of course there's no manual you asshole! What do you think this is? A labored metaphor about the foibles of modern life?

DEAD. Okay why, then?

GOD. Alright, you want the truth?

DEAD. Are you going to hurt my feelings again?

GOD. Nah.

DEAD. Then yes.

GOD. Alright … how can I put this? Hmm … much in the same way you were pulled out of the primordial soup of the universe and given form, I was brought into existence by an external force without my knowledge or my consent. I, like you, am not here by choice but I am, nevertheless, here. My motivations, lacking the guiding impetus of a greater purpose toward which to direct my actions, are purely of my own invention.

DEAD. Okay, that doesn't really answer my -

GOD. Let me finish. At first I couldn't empathize with your kind because all you seemed to care about was eating, sleeping, and sex. Which, fair play, those are some of my best works. I got resentful, hence the Black Death, Earthquakes, and all those plagues in Egypt. I was really leaning into the whole Christianity thing back then, gave me sort of a god complex … oh shit, THAT'S where that phrase comes from!

DEAD. Jesus Christ -

GOD. *(Laughing.)* Can't believe that never occurred to me before.

DEAD. You're just a psychopath!

GOD. Oh yeah, this coming from a member of a species

that pathologically hates itself so much it can't stop bickering over what color your skin should be for long enough to stop the planet boiling over and imploding! I made a bunch of different colors because I like variety, okay?! If I had known it would cause like fifty major atrocities I woulda just kept you all brown!

DEAD. Alright jeez, just … just calm down for a sec. I have one more question …

GOD. Okay but hurry up, we got like two minutes before the alien thing wears off and people start blaming the government for their problems again.

DEAD. If you hate humanity so much, why are you so concerned about what happens to us?

GOD. What? I don't hate humanity!

DEAD. Seriously? Because it really seems like that's bullshit. What kind of loving god would allow so much suffering to exist in the world unless it resented our existence so much it wanted to do its best to snuff us out? *(God stands and moves toward the window.)*

GOD. Come here, let me show you something. Look down there, tell me what you see.

DEAD. It's Earth. Just really tiny.

GOD. Look closer … here let me zoom in. See that?

DEAD. Oh …

GOD. Yeah … you ever have kids when you were alive?

DEAD. No … I never figured that out before I …

GOD. The point is, I may disagree with a lot of your choices … well that's putting it lightly … I may be utterly fucking flabbergasted by the shit you people choose to do, but ultimately you are as I have made you, imperfect. All that you are is what I am, and all that I am is what you are. The only mistake your kind ever made was dressing me up to be some kind of entity that was beyond sentimentality and folly. To finish answering your question … once I realized that you were only flawed because of what I had done to you, it became clear to me that your survival and, ideally your prosperity, was equal to the essence of my existence. If you all fail, so will I. If I ever hope to reconcile my hectic existence with some kind of grander purpose, some kind of end, I have to accept that I am as much a product of you as you are a product of me. Maybe I made some fucked up choices in the past, but it is what it is. It's not like there's some kind of metaphysical control Z.

DEAD. Wow I … I never thought of it that way.

GOD. Yeah well, most people don't. *(Beat.)* You alright?

DEAD. I'm … processing. *(God nods and exits.)* Man … I could really use a … *(God enters holding two beers and hands one to Dead Person.)* … a beer … You read my mind.

GOD. If only I could … that would make this whole thing a lot easier. *(They sit and open their beers, drinking silently for a beat. At some point, both God and Dead Person do something that unintentionally mirrors the other. They notice this and share a brief laugh about it.)*

DEAD. So … was my life … meaningless?

GOD. You tell me. *(A raucous uproar of voices rising up in a riot.)*

DEAD. Uh … should you, do something about that?

GOD. Nah, they probably just found out about another human rights crime somewhere in Asia. They'll forget about it in three … two … one … *(Sounds of people booing and jeering.)*

DEAD. What was that?

GOD. Another comedian said a slur on TV.

DEAD. Oh.

GOD. Alright, I've got a question for you now.

DEAD. Shoot.

WHAT THE HELL IS GOING ON? by Julian Diaz

GOD. First, were you religious in life?

DEAD. Nah. Who's got that kind of time?

GOD. But you weren't ever certain whether you were right about there being a god.

DEAD. I guess so. I mean, it's impossible to know for sure what happens after you die.

GOD. So, if you knew what you know now, would that really have changed how you lived your life?

DEAD. … I mean –

GOD. Does knowing for sure that it all ends in nothingness make you want to have … I don't know … been a serial killer?

DEAD. What? No, why would I want to be a murderer just because there's no … Oh … I see.

GOD. Life is only meaningless if you let it be. Just because it wasn't set in stone at the conception of the universe doesn't make it any less valid.

DEAD. Hey … thanks God.

GOD. Don't mention it.

DEAD. *(Beat.)* So … Now what? Should you go back to running the world?

GOD. Yeah … eventually. If I don't fuck with them for a while they start getting comfortable and inventing weird shit like almond milk and eightteen different TV shows just about cake.

DEAD. And … what should I do?

GOD. Uh … you want another beer?

DEAD. Yeah, fuck it. *(God moves to get another beer but stops. Distant nuclear sirens.)*

GOD. Oh god dammit!

DEAD. What?

GOD. They're trying to kill each other again …

DEAD. What are they fighting over this time?

GOD. Uh let's see … huh … apparently the liberal agenda did involve killing all the straight white republicans.

DEAD. I fucking knew it.

END OF PLAY

WHY DID YOU BOTHER KILLING THE SEA WITCH?

By Jenna Jane

The little mermaid and her prince realize they're not going to sail off into the sunset together after all. (Comedy, 1M, 1W)

CHARACTERS

MERMAID
Female, teens to mid-20s. Earnest, genuine, naïve, inexperienced, totally out of her element. Believes the world is a great adventure. Tries too hard.

PRINCE
Male, mid-20s to mid-30s. Practical, brooding, sick of having to live up to others' expectations.

SETTING

Onboard Prince's ship.

NOTES

On gender references, these are only suggestions. Gender is just a performative social construct, anyway. Do whatever feels right to you.

***

At rise, Mermaid and Prince stand side-by-side, down center, looking off into the distance and breathing heavily. This should last about 10 seconds. We hear seagulls screeching and waves splashing. Prince looks exhausted. Mermaid looks like she has enough energy to perform every role in an entire musical right

85

fucking now. They are both head-to-toe soaking wet.

MERMAID. *(Abruptly.)* Wow! That was amazing! *(She starts pacing and waving her arms around, reenacting the battle. Prince sits down on the ground with a splat and sighs. He puts his head in his hands. He's just trying to catch his breath.)* I mean, you did it! You defeated the evil sea witch! You were like, POW! And then you were like, BAM! And then you were like, DIE, EVIL SEA WITCH, DIE! *(She laughs. Prince sighs with exhaustion.)* And now, my handsome prince, we can get married and live happily ever after!

PRINCE. *(His head snaps up to look at her.)* I'm sorry, did you say "married?"

MERMAID. Of course! That's why you defeated the evil sea witch – so we can sail off into the sunset together as king and queen! You're the prince charming I've always dreamed of.

PRINCE. You mean, these past few days that we've been hanging out – this whole time you were trying to … seduce me? *(An uncomfortable pause with constant eye contact.)* Whoa. I feel really objectified right now.

MERMAID. *(Bewildered.)* What?

PRINCE. I just feel like you're totally objectifying me. I thought we were friends. *(Mermaid sits down on the ground next to him with her legs out to the side, knees together, weight on one hip.)*

MERMAID. I don't understand. Objectifying you – how? I'm in love with you. I gave up being a mermaid to be with you.

PRINCE Even if you used to have fins, you're just like every other princess I've ever met. All you princesses ever see is a pretty face, biceps and a palace.

MERMAID. *(Reaches out to touch his bicep, then pulls her hand back abruptly.)* That's not true!

PRINCE. You don't know anything about me. What do you even like about me?

MERMAID. Well, you're … *(Uncomfortable pause. Mermaid wrings out her hair. She's trying to think.)* Brave? You … defeated the sea witch? You have … *(Prince shakes some water out of his hair.)* Nice hair?

PRINCE. *(Deadpan. His hair looks shit.)* I'm brave and have nice hair. *(Mermaid nods.)* You don't even know my middle name. As a matter of fact, what's my last name?

MERMAID. Prince … *(She blows air out one side of her mouth.)* Smith? *(Prine stands and steps away from her. He adjusts his wet clothes, uncomfortably.)*

PRINCE. You realize this is the first conversation we've ever had, right? You just got your voice back, like 20 minutes ago. You think I'm so shallow that I'd marry someone I've never had a conversation with? What's your 5-year plan? What's your 10-year plan?

MERMAID. My what?

PRINCE. How old are you?

MERMAID. Sixteen.

PRINCE. Sixteen?! *(Mermaid stands and adjusts her wet clothes.)*

MERMAID. *(Defensively.)* Sixteen!

PRINCE. I'm 28! You're 16! That doesn't seem, I don't know, creepy to you?

MERMAID. Why is everyone always screaming at me that I'm only 16? First Daddy, now you?

PRINCE. *(Trying to adjust his wet pants.)* I'm not interested in any part of your Daddy issues. *(Shaking out his wet hair again. He's uncomfortable and frustrated.)* Gaaah, I'm so damp!

MERMAID. *(Wringing out her dress.)* Water is so much more unpleasant with clothes on!

PRINCE. Well, there's a line I've never heard before.

MERMAID. Why did you bother killing the sea witch if you're not in love with me? I thought we had an unspoken connection!

PRINCE *(As if it's the only possible answer.)* What else do you do with a sea witch?!

MERMAID. Look, I saved your life! When you were on this very ship, and that big storm hit, and you fell overboard.

PRINCE. *(Pauses fussing with his wet clothes.)* That was you?

MERMAID. I rescued you! I dragged you to shore and sang at you until you regained consciousness. *(She faces the audience, takes a step or two down stage, puts her hands over her heart, and inhales. She is about to sing.)*

PRINCE. Don't!

MERMAID. What?

PRINCE. Please don't!

MERMAID. Don't … sing?

PRINCE. Don't sing!

MERMAID. Why not?

PRINCE. I remember what happened now. I woke up covered in sand, the sun was in my eyes, a woman was hovering over me, belting. To be honest, it was … pitchy.

MERMAID. Bitchy?!

PRINCE. *(Overemphasizing the p's.)* Pitchy. With a "P." Like pineapple. Or please don't sing.

MERMAID. *(Genuinely hurt and confused.)* But I saved your life! You would have drowned!

PRINCE. So, what, that means you're entitled to me now? Romantically?

MERMAID. No, that's not what I -

PRINCE. Sexually?

MERMAID. You've got this all wrong -

PRINCE. I didn't ask you to rescue me. I didn't ask you to stop wearing clams on your tits. Now, you think I owe you something? A marriage? Offspring?

MERMAID. I rescued you because I loved you at first sight!

PRINCE. Because you objectified me the moment you saw me.

MERMAID. Because I thought we would be compatible!

PRINCE. Are you a dog person? Because that's a non-negotiable for me.

MERMAID. *(Beyond frustrated and confused.)* What's a dog?!

PRINCE. *(Slowly, trying to find the words.)* It's a pet. An animal companion.

MERMAID. I've only ever had crabs!

PRINCE. *(Pause. Realizes she means crustaceans. Changes the subject.)* What are your hobbies? What do you do for fun?

MERMAID. Well, I collect things.

PRINCE. You collect things.

MERMAID. Human things.

PRINCE. *(Getting more creeped out by the second.)* Human things.

MERMAID. Artifacts. Candelabras, marble busts, and -

PRINCE. First of all, I do not want a hoarder in my palace. I am a minimalist, which you would know if you bothered to try to get to know me beyond "he has nice hair."

MERMAID. *(She reaches for his bicep again, catches herself, pulls back.)* What's a hoarder?

PRINCE. Second, I'm not just another human artifact to add to your collection. I'm not an object for you to look at and admire. *(He looks down, then out at the audience, broodingly.)* I have feelings. I have thoughts.

MERMAID. When I looked up at you from the waves for the first time, standing at the wheel of this ship, I knew you were an explorer like me. All I've ever wanted was to see the world – the human world. I've already explored under the sea, now I'm ready to spread my legs and explore the surface.

PRINCE. That's not really the right phrase for –

MERMAID

(Not listening. Lost in her vision of their life together.)

We'll sail from land to land together, king and queen explorers. We'll discover new cultures, travel to all the great wonders of the world, see all the –

PRINCE. I don't want any of that.

MERMAID. *(Blindsided.)* What do you mean?

PRINCE. I don't want to explore the world.

MERMAID. But I saw you! On this very ship -

PRINCE. I wasn't out exploring the world. I just like being on a boat.

MERMAID. I don't understand.

PRINCE. The constraints of governing at the palace – it's all so tedious. Sometimes, it's nice to just shirk the mundane responsibilities of the crown, leave the taxation and infrastructure improvements to someone else, and head out to sea.

MERMAID. But you must be traveling somewhere on this ship, right? You must be going somewhere.

PRINCE. Nope.

MERMAID. You just want to be on a boat.

PRINCE. Exactly.

MERMAID. And you don't want to get off the boat.

PRINCE. Right.

MERMAID. You don't want to explore or sightsee. You just want to be on a boat, floating on the water, far away from your royal subjects and fancy palace.

PRINCE. *(As if truly seeing her for the first time.)* Wow. You do get me.

MERMAID. Look, I didn't leave my enormous family, diverse friend group, and my own fancy palace to hang out on a boat for the rest of my life. I traded in my tail for feet. And I intend to use them for more than walking from bow to stern.

PRINCE. Sounds like we're finally on the same page.

MERMAID. Well, shit.

PRINCE. Welcome to the young adult genre.

MERMAID. It's not going to work between us.

PRINCE. That's what I've been saying this whole time.

MERMAID. Just because you're a prince and I'm a princess, that doesn't make us a good match.

PRINCE. Couldn't agree more.

MERMAID. I don't want to be part of your world.

PRINCE. Best we go our separate ways, then.

MERMAID. Appreciate you killing the sea witch, though.

PRINCE. Didn't have much of a choice. *(Mermaid approaches the lip of the stage, gets ready to dive, then stops herself.)*

MERMAID. I have no idea how to swim with legs.

PRINCE. You're asking the guy who almost drowned?

MERMAID. *(Sighs, looks out at the audience.)* Adulting sucks.

END OF PLAY

9 781737 521679